5/20/2017

Jessie,

Thank you so much
for your friendship and
support. I hope you enjoy
Compass Rose, and all the
novels to come!

Elizabeth Austin

XOXO.

Compass Rose

by Elizabeth Austin

Compass Rose

Text © 2017 by Elizabeth Austin
Cover and Interior Art by Matias G. Martinez

Email: publisher@radionmedia.com.
www.hypatiaeducation.com
www.radionmedia.com

Print ISBN-10: 1-946496-04-9, 13:978-1-946496-04-1

Ebook ISBN-10: 1-946496-05-7, 13: 978-1-946496-05-8

First Edition

Acknowledgements

This is my first novel and writing it was both an academic and emotional process from which I learned more about myself than I had anticipated. Thank you to the incredible team at Radion Media, especially Editor-in-Chief Risa Peris, for publishing Compass Rose. You believed in me and this novel, and for that I will be forever grateful. My network of supportive friends and family who read portions of my manuscript deserve more praise and thanks than I can express here. You know who you are and I am grateful. Particular thanks to Amanda Lehmberg, David Janett, and Emily Thompson for their detailed notes and edits; and thanks to my brothers, David and Christopher, for their support. Above all, thank you to my loving, intelligent, strong and articulate parents and grandparents: Cathy Kiselyak Austin, Milton Austin, Carol Harper, and Chuck Kiselyak. Thank you for giving me everything I needed to pursue my dreams while supporting myself. No matter how far I roam, I know I can always come home.

Introduction

She was staring at the gate. It was made of iron. Her breathing was shallow. She could feel the edges of her dress, wet with mud, brushing against her calves. She had picked this dress from a window in a shop while on a walk with her father four years ago. It was when her life had been peaceful, before the revolution. It was a spring day. The breeze was coming in from the valley so she had worn a scarf. She was holding her father's hand as they had often done when she was a child. She didn't remember why she had reached for his hand that day though she was glad now that she had. It had become a memory she held onto in her darkest moments, when the world no longer was full of possibilities and she felt the walls of inferiority closing in around her.

When they had come for her family she was not home. She was visiting her aunt. She had not heard the pleading cries of her mother, or the shots fired near her brothers' heads to keep them from coming any closer to the soldiers. She did not know what her father had said to the men who took him or if he had struggled. She had tried to imagine the scenario when she first heard the news but as the years passed she tried to forget it. All her memories had been whittled down to just this one — the strength she felt holding her father's hand as they walked down the street.

Emily's Story

Four years ago

The House

It was quiet. The air was still. She was sitting on the floor in her room. The house was empty. It had been three weeks since the revolutionaries had taken her family. The furniture had been looted, the food long rotted, but there were a few things still left in her room. A couple of day dresses, a comb, an old pair of winter boots, and her notebooks which she had kept locked in the lower drawer of her bureau. She picked a notebook at random and opened it to the first page.

"Once upon a time there was a girl who was loved very well. Her name was Emily."

She stared at the words, the notebook open in her lap.

She had never kept a traditional diary but several notebooks where she wrote down whatever she liked or felt was important; stories, poems, observations. She had written this entry in third person and reading it she wondered if she still was that Emily. The girl who wrote them was very different from the one reading them now.

"She was tall for her age and shy about it. She had raven hair that turned auburn in the sun like her grandmother's. She had green eyes but her family didn't know where they had come from. Emily told them they had come from God. She wasn't sure how much she didn't know about the world but she was confident in what she knew. Emily loved facts."

She had written those words seven years ago when she was thirteen. In her young mind her life had seemed complex but it hadn't been. She knew that now.

"Emily had two brothers, Daniel and Wallace. Daniel was ten years old and Wallace was eight years old. Wallace followed Emily everywhere."

She could still see her brothers at those ages, especially Wallace who would crawl into bed with her when he had nightmares. They were different now. Wallace had turned fifteen last month and was taller than father. She hoped he hadn't tried to fight the soldiers. He could be so headstrong. Daniel was clever. He would have gone with them and then secretly escaped in the middle of the night. But what if he hadn't? What if he had been caught? What if he had tried to stop Wallace from fighting and they both had been killed? These questions ran through Emily's mind constantly. The day the men came she was visiting her Aunt Caroline for lunch. She had worn the new dress father had bought her the day before.

Aunt Caroline lived in a large, old house just over a mile away. She was Emily's father's sister and a widow. Her husband had died young. Aunt Caroline was tall, like Emily, but with wider hips and a thicker waist. Her hair was light brown with flecks of gray. After her husband died, she had formed an attachment to Emily. Sometimes love lost disappears, and other times it has to find somewhere to go. Whenever Emily was home from university Aunt Caroline insist-

ed she come over for lunch. Emily was only home for a long weekend but she obliged. That morning was the last time she had seen
her family. She remembered the smell of coffee brewing, and her
father's voice bellowing down the stairs.

"Catherine! I can't find my blue tie. Remember it? I just got it from
Mom."

"Try looking with the dry cleaning, Jack," her mother replied. Her
voice had a melodic quality. Every note was crystal clear and linked
to the next phrase like a song.

Emily was sitting at the kitchen table. She was in her pajamas, her
knees pulled up to her chest and her feet resting on the seat of the
chair. She was watching her mother pour three cups of coffee. Her
father came downstairs wearing a red tie.

"I couldn't find it," he said gruffly.

"Why do you have to meet the governor on a Saturday anyway?"
her mother asked.

"There's been some more trouble with the rebels in the north. He
wants us to explore some legal options. If this all goes to shit, he
doesn't want to end up at The Hague."

"It won't get that bad, will it? I thought they were just protesting.
On the news they made it sound like a couple fringe groups, not a
formal revolution."

"Probably not, but these groups are popping up all over. You just
need to recite that manifesto and all of a sudden you're a conscript-
ed revolutionary, waving that ridiculous flag."

"How long do you think it will take?"

"Couple of hours. We're not drafting any documents just exploring options. I should be home by two or three o'clock, no later."

Emily turned to gaze out of the window as her parents talked. It was a bright, clear day. The trees were still leafless but the grass was green and the perennials were starting to bloom. When she looked back her father was gone. She heard his footsteps as he walked down the hall toward the front door. She heard the front door open and close and then, silence. Not the silence of an empty house but household silence. There is a difference. The low humming of machines, the creak of wood floors, the ticking of a kitchen timer. It means there is life in the house.

Her mother placed two cups of coffee on the table and sat down across from her.

"Well you have lunch at twelve with Aunt Caroline and then what are your plans for the rest of the day?"

"I think Wallace and I might go see a movie tonight. Not sure. He's not up yet but we talked about it yesterday."

"What about Daniel?"

"He said he's hanging out with some friends."

"Okay, well I have some laundry to do and I want to run some errands before your father gets home, but tomorrow let's spend some time together. Maybe take a walk at that new park?"

"Sure."

Her mother smiled.

And that was it. The last time she had spoken to her mother. Emily had sipped her coffee and started reading the newspaper, and her mother had left the kitchen.

Emily's eyes darted to the door. She heard a sound. Were the soldiers back? She quickly stood up and peered out of the doorway and down the hall. Nothing. Silence again. She leaned out of the door and saw it, a stray cat. She breathed a sigh of relief but realized how long she had been in her room. She went back to the bureau and took two dresses and two notebooks, stuffing them in her knapsack. She slipped on the winter boots and threw the sandals she'd been wearing in the corner. Quietly she made her way down the stairs and out of the house, not knowing if she would ever return.

The Journey

For the first time in three weeks Emily had a purpose, other than staying alive, and a destination. She was going to a refugee camp. After the rebels had moved on, people started to come out of hiding, including Emily. She was living in the woods. Every night she would venture out from her hiding place, a hollowed out tree she covered in brush, and go in search of food. She was lucky. Most of the town was deserted. People had fled as soon as they heard gunfire. She went into empty houses and took whatever was left in their cupboards. She was too afraid to stay in any one house very long, but remained well fed and relatively clean.

During the day she would curl up in the corner of the hollowed out tree, her knees to her chest, and try to make herself as small as possible. Flickers of sunlight would come in through the brush but she was careful to always stay back, in the dark. She heard birds chirping outside, interspersed with distant gunfire. Finally, two days ago, the gunfire had stopped. And today she made it out in daylight.

On her way to her old house she had come across one of her aunt's neighbors. An older woman named Ruth who had been hiding in her own cellar. She spoke in short, blunt clips and her voice was eerily detached from her words. Ruth said she had heard on the radio that the government was setting up a refugee camp "northwest of here, near Lansing." Ruth said she wasn't going. This was her town and she was staying put. Emily knew she had to go. She needed protection and if her family had survived, they might be there.

When she had escaped from her aunt's house into the woods, she had left her belongings behind. Since then she collected supplies, including the knapsack to carry them in, from the different houses she looted. Emily had a compass, a kitchen knife, a pair of scissors, a flashlight, a lighter, and a reusable water bottle. She walked down to the end of the street, closer to the woods, and took out the compass.

She looked down at the compass and its wavering arrow.

"The needle always points north," she said softly to herself. She turned the dial. "So west is…" she looked up, the river was west of here and that was where the compass was pointing. Emily smiled. Lansing was less than a week's walking distance away and she had enough food for two or three days. She was hoping to come across more abandoned houses where she could get supplies. She didn't want her knapsack to get too heavy though.

Survival skills were something Emily had only a cursory knowledge of, from her father and her brothers. They loved being outdoors. Hiking, camping, fishing, these were activities the Caring men enjoyed. When Emily was younger, and her brothers were too small to do much, her father used to lecture her on these skills and their significance – how to tie a knot, how to build a fire, how important it is to stay hydrated. Like all men, her father had done his mandatory year of military service before university. He had served abroad, in areas where fresh water was scarce and infrastructure had been destroyed. The knowledge he was trying to impart was important, but until now Emily hadn't seen how it was relevant. She hadn't lived through a war. It seemed to her that the only times you needed these skills were when you voluntary subjected yourself to the elements. If you didn't, you could just live a life where fire came from the gas stove in the kitchen and water was readily available from the tap. Knot tying had no purpose; tying your shoes was enough.

The first night on the road, Emily stayed in an abandoned warehouse just off the highway. It was one large room, roughly half the size of a football field, with a lofted space that probably used to be an office. As she climbed the stairs to the loft she saw it, a nearly full water cooler in the corner of the room. This was incredible. Filtered, clean water just waiting for her. She climbed the last few stairs, knelt down at the water cooler and re-filled her near empty bottle. Waves of relief swept over her. She would be hydrated tomorrow.

Using her knapsack as a pillow, Emily stretched out on the bare, wooden floor and started to drift off to sleep. Seconds after she closed her eyes an image flashed through her mind. Blood, creeping slowly along the floor, inching toward the staircase where Emily stood on the third step, looking down at it. Her eyes snapped open. She felt a weight in her chest. Her breathing was labored. Aunt Caroline. She had blocked this image from her mind but here it was, vivid.

She had been just about to leave Aunt Caroline's when the soldiers came. She had been coming back downstairs from using the bathroom. There was a pounding at the front door as she was walking down the hall to the staircase. Then Aunt Caroline's voice saying something she couldn't decipher and a deep, male voice barking at her, "Caring, we're looking for Emily Caring. John Caring's daughter." Emily froze. She had never experienced the feeling that came over her next. It was danger, fear, and nausea in one intense jolt that hit her stomach and then filled her body. If this was fight or flight her mind was screaming "flight!"

She peered down the stairs. The light from the front door was just visible and she heard her aunt saying, "She's not here."

"You're lying!" the man barked and then Emily heard the sound of a blunt object hitting bone, and the collapse of a body onto the floor. "You two go around back, I'll go into the house. She's probably hiding back there." Emily pulled herself back into the hallway until she heard heavy footsteps traveling to the back of the house. They weren't coming upstairs, yet.

She took one step down the stairs and saw her aunt's blood creeping toward the staircase. What happened next wasn't clear in her memory. It was only there in flashing images. Nothing was linear or coherent. She remembered feeling for her aunt's pulse on her neck and hearing gunfire in the distance. She remembered running through the woods, searching for a place to hide. And she remembered seeing the hollowed-out tree. The moments tying those events together were blank.

She sat up in the lofted room and tried to measure her breathing.

"Hello?" A young, male voice echoed in the warehouse. "Hello? Is anyone in here?"

Emily crawled to the doorway and peered out into the warehouse. She couldn't see the young man's face since his flashlight was too bright, but he was wearing jeans and sneakers, not a military uniform and combat boots. The flashlight swept up to the loft and Emily leaned back behind the door.

"Who are you?" her own voice surprised her. It was strong, blunt, and in her lower register.

"Hello! Someone is here. I knew it. I have a sense for these things. Are you up there in the office?"

"You didn't answer my question. Who are you?"

"Oh yes, sorry. I'm Ben. Benjamin Hughes. The revolutionaries attacked the town I was in so I've been on the road for a few days. I assume that's why you're hiding. Don't worry I won't hurt you."

"How do you know I'm not a revolutionary? I'm armed." Emily was moving to the knapsack to get the scissors.

"Okay, sure. Yes. I suppose you could be a revolutionary but I'm telling you I'm not one. That makes me pretty vulnerable if you are one, so maybe give me the benefit of the doubt? Or not. I get that. I'm just trying to find somewhere to sleep tonight. I can stay down here and you can stay up there, or you can come down and introduce yourself."

Emily thought for a minute. A month ago she would have gone down. Now she wasn't sure. He was already here though so even if she didn't go down and meet him, he could always come up and attack her. There was only one door in and out of the warehouse that she knew of.

"All right. I'm coming down. Don't move and don't shine your flashlight in my face."

Emily swung her knapsack over her shoulder and took her flashlight out of the side pocket. She shined the light down and out into the warehouse as she walked down the stairs to meet Ben. When she got closer to him she saw that he was built kind of like Wallace, tall with broad shoulders. He had dark skin and dark eyes. She got within a few feet of him.

"I'm Emily. Emily…" she stopped herself. She was afraid to say her last name, "Johnson." It was her aunt's married name.

"Hi Emily Johnson, it's nice to meet you." Ben smiled. He was just a man, not a predator.

"It's nice to meet you too."

"So, how long have you been up there?"

"Oh I just got here today, well tonight. There's some filtered water up there, if you want some."

"Really? That would be great, thanks. Man you really lucked out. Clean water and this whole place all to yourself? Well, until I got here that is." Ben chuckled. "Sorry if I scared you." He really did remind her of Wallace. His mannerisms, the way he shrugged his shoulders when he laughed.

"So, you've been on the road for a few days?"

"Yeah, three days. I'm heading down south to Elkhart. My cousins live there. I heard it's safer now, in the south." Emily nodded. She didn't have any cousins. Aunt Caroline never had children and her mother was an only child. "How about you?" he asked.

"I'm heading to Lansing."

"Gotcha. You have family there?"

Emily paused, the question made her nauseous, "I might. Listen, I'll probably still sleep up there and I'd prefer it if you stay down here. You can get the water first, if you want."

"I can just get the water in the morning, no worries."

He paused. Emily nodded again.

"Okay then. I will see you in the morning."

"See you in the morning."

As she made her way back up to the loft her loneliness was palpable. She didn't want to be alone, but she didn't want to be with a stranger either. She wanted to be with her family.

In the morning, the sunlight came in brightly from the window above where Emily was sleeping. It warmed her face. She wasn't dreaming exactly but she felt safe and comforted by its warmth as she awoke. It took her almost a minute to be fully awake and to remember where she was. She rose slowly and walked over to the door to the loft. Ben was sitting in the center of the warehouse heating something over a camping stove. She could smell coffee.

"Good morning," her voice was softer.

"Morning, you sleep okay?"

"Yes, thank you. I did. You?"

"Yeah, I can pretty much sleep anywhere. I used to fall asleep in the car all the time as a kid." He chuckled again. "Want some breakfast? I've got coffee and oatmeal."

"Sure, thanks. That's really nice of you."

"Of course, we revolutionaries have to stick together."

Emily froze.

"It was a joke. Man you must have really been through something."

"Haven't you?"

"Not really," he shrugged. "I was up north for a job interview. My parents live abroad, and the only family I have around here are my cousins. I was staying with them for a week doing interviews around here. You'd think more people would need to hire engineers with all the construction they're doing, but the competition is stiff. Anyway, they said it was going to be more peaceful protests but something was off. I'm telling you, I get a feeling about these things. Sure enough, within twenty-four hours all hell breaks loose and I end up on the road. My phone is dead now but I was able to call my parents and tell them I'm okay. I'll call them again when I get back to Elkhart. This country isn't what it used to be, that's for sure, but what do the revolutionaries want with me? I was born here, sure, but I didn't grow up here and my parents don't work for the government. Some job interview week. Man, I am never coming back here again."

He made it sound so simple; matter of fact. It had happened and he had moved on. Emily had never considered that not everyone was as traumatized as she was. Her father did work for the government and pretty high up in the governor's administration. He wasn't a criminal though, and neither was anyone else in her family. The rebels didn't even know her father. He was kind and compassionate, not some lethal monster or government drone.

Emily shifted uncomfortably and then sat down on the floor, next to the camping stove.

"Okay, here you go." Ben passed her a mug of coffee and another mug of oatmeal with a spoon in it. "Sorry I don't have any milk or anything; you'll have to take it black."

"That's okay. Thank you... again." Emily sipped her coffee in silence, not sure what to say. She didn't want to talk about her life, and she wasn't sure how much more she wanted to know about Ben's. His future seemed so much brighter than hers.

"So... want to hear a joke?" Ben asked.

"Oh, uh yeah. Sure."

He smiled. She liked his smile, it was warm and sincere.

"Okay, what starts with E, ends with E, and only has one letter?"

"Hmm... I don't know."

"An envelope."

Emily smiled. She wasn't expecting that. It was simple, fun.

"Oh you like that? I've got a million of them. My grandfather gave me this book when I was ten and I memorized them. Have you heard the joke about the butter?"

"What? No, I haven't. What is it?"

"I better not tell you, it might spread."

"Wow. That's terrible!" Emily said, smiling wider.

"Okay, one more, what did one wall say to the other?"

"What?"

"I'll meet you at the corner."

Then she laughed, and her light-hearted laughter echoed in the warehouse. It was strange. Two days ago she was hiding in a tree, and now she was here, in this warehouse, with a person she barely knew, laughing at corny, grade school jokes. But it worked, somehow. Life made sense in that moment.

After they had finished breakfast, Ben gathered his things and packed them carefully in his backpack. He went upstairs to fill his water bottle, and when he came back down Emily was standing too. He looked at her cautiously.

"Since you're heading north to Lansing, and I'm heading south to Elkhart, I guess it doesn't make sense for us to travel together. I could walk with you for a little while, though, if you need the company?"

Emily thought for a minute. Did she? "No, I'm okay. Thanks again for breakfast."

"All right," he said, shifting his weight. "Well I'll give you my number and the number at my cousins' house in case you need anything later on. I should be there sometime next week."

"Okay, sure."

He took out a piece of paper and a pen, scratched down the numbers and handed the paper to her.

"Thanks."

"Anytime, well goodbye then, Emily Johnson. It was very nice to meet you."

"Bye." Emily watched him walk away until she was alone in the warehouse.

——-

The next two days on the road went by slowly. She didn't know any back paths to Lansing, only the highways. Since Lansing was central, highways ran to and from it. In the car these routes had been quick; on foot they were tedious, grueling. The highways were surrounded by open, unending farmland. Not a house in sight.

As she walked, her mind mulled over one topic and then the next. The migrations of birds. The feudal system. Curtains she had picked for her old dorm room. She replayed an entire album's worth of songs in her head by bands her parents liked and had played in the house. Sometimes her mind would wander, floating without focus, and other times it would hone in on a certain memory. Her second night on the road, she slept in a barn which overlooked a river and was reminded of when Wallace had named their family dog.

She and her brothers had begged for a dog for years and finally, when Wallace was eleven, her parents had relented. The trip to the animal shelter was taken just by Wallace, mother, and Emily. Father had to work, and Daniel, increasingly less interested in family activities, chose to stay home. This was when Wallace was still pretty attached to them, but mother knew it wouldn't last much longer. She had seen it with Daniel. In a couple years Wallace would withdraw, and she was hoping that the dog would be some comfort to him in his teenage years, when he no longer wanted to share his feelings with his family.

As they walked down the row of cages at the shelter, some dogs jumped up, others slept.

Mother took a liking to a small, light brown Yorkshire Terrier. "What about this one? He seems friendly," she said, bringing her hand up to the cage so the dog could sniff it.

"No, not that one," Wallace said, pausing, "there's one in here that's a Caring, I just know it. Let's keep going."

Emily smiled to herself. "A Caring," he knew that family had a certain feeling.

Then he stopped in front of a cage with a black Staffordshire Terrier. The dog was jumping up, its paws rattling the cage door. Wallace called a shelter worker over.

"Would you like to take her for a walk?"

Wallace looked at mother, who answered the shelter worker. "No, we'd like to take her home."

The worker opened the cage door and slipped a collar, with a leash attached, around the dog's neck. The dog jumped on Wallace, her head desperately reaching up to lick his face. Wallace smiled and held her paws for a moment until she descended.

"What do you want to name her?" Emily asked.

He thought for a moment. "River."

"Why River?"

Emily was expecting some Lord of the Rings character or goddess from Greek mythology; both subjects Wallace loved and when asked, would explain their nuances in detail.

"Because, well, rivers are everything really. When we're out camping with dad he talks about them all the time. You can get water from them, catch fish in them, and bathe in them. They're a major source of life. And I think that since she's a Caring, she deserves a name that means something to us."

Emily thought about how different Wallace's life was supposed to be right now. She didn't know what had happened to River; if she had fled the house or if the rebels had simply shot her. She hoped it was the former, of course, but that's not what filled her mind. Wallace was only fifteen. These were the years that mother had planned for, when he would withdraw from the family and need a dog for comfort when his words failed him. All that was over now. His life was forever changed. He no longer had the luxury of an adolescence.

The third night on the road Emily saw an exit sign for a town called

Mason. She hadn't been there before, but she knew it was a small town. She was apprehensive. On the one hand, the revolutionaries could be there. She didn't hear gunfire or see any lights in the distance, but that didn't mean they weren't lurking somewhere nearby. On the other hand, she was running low on food and water. She decided to risk it. Without nourishment she would be dead anyway.

The exit led onto Mason's main street. It was clear the town had seen violence. Several cars were overturned, and some had been torched. Of the ten or so lampposts she could see, only two were lit. The others had shattered bulbs. She veered off onto a side street with a row of houses. It was a new development, every house had the same design but each was its own version of damaged. Some had shutters hanging off the hinges; others had missing front doors and broken windows. Toys and pieces of furniture littered the front yards. Emily thought she saw movement in an upper window of a house on her left. She glanced up, but no one was there.

At the end of the block were a few small, older houses. Their damage was less significant and Emily hoped there would be more food and supplies left inside. There was one house in particular that stood out, not because of any specific characteristic, but because it reminded her of her friend Annabelle's house. Emily had known Annabelle since the third grade. Her house had the same shutters, cobbled walkway, and front porch as this house in Mason. Emily had spent countless nights there catching fireflies and having sleepovers, until high school when they had drifted apart due to varying interests and social cliques. She hadn't spoken to Annabelle since high school graduation. She hadn't thought about Annabelle until this moment. Now she missed her, and the simplicity of childhood.

She approached the house from the side, looking in the windows first. A dining room chair was overturned, but nothing seemed broken. She circled back to the front of the house, walked up the porch steps, hesitated slightly, and then opened the front door. She shined her flashlight into the house. The front door opened into a long hallway. She took two steps in and swept her flashlight left and then right. On the left was a sitting area, on the right was the dining room. She walked further into the house. There was a bathroom and the kitchen was at the end of the hallway.

As she entered the kitchen she sensed movement at her feet. She swung her flashlight down and saw the tails of two mice as they scampered away. She shined her flashlight back up and saw several open cupboards along the back wall. Not much was left in them. On the bottom shelf there were mouse droppings and a box of crackers which had been gnawed open. On the second shelf there was an unopened jar of peanut butter, and two cans of tuna fish. She reached up, took the items down from the second shelf and put them in her knapsack.

She discovered a staircase and walked up the steps slowly, carefully. She wasn't sure what she would find up there. Squirrels? Raccoons? Instead she found two small rooms. One with a bed, lamp, desk, and chair, and the other had several book shelves lining the walls. Something about sleeping in someone else's bed made her uneasy, so instead of sleeping in the bed, she took the comforter off the bed and laid it out on the floor of the room with the books. She had eaten earlier in the day, and was exhausted, so she stretched out on the comforter and quickly fell asleep.

A couple hours later, Emily felt something nudging her leg. She was half asleep and didn't quite register what was nudging her. She rolled over onto her side and opened her eyes. She froze. A figure was standing above her, casting a shadow from inside the doorway. She looked down at her feet. A combat boot was next to her ankle; it nudged her again.

"Get up."

She stood up slowly, taking in the soldier as she rose. He wore military fatigues, not a formal uniform. He was armed with one standard, automatic rifle. The kind her father was issued when he served his mandatory year. He might have other weapons that she couldn't see, but he was resting the rifle in his arm. When she was standing upright, she looked up at his face. He was several inches taller than she was, in his early forties and clean cut. He didn't look directly at her; instead he looked right above her head.

"Who are you and why are you staying here? We cleared this town last week, there are to be no civilians in this area."

"I'm passing through on my way to Lansing."

He looked down at her. "Why?"

She didn't reply. She didn't know if she should say she was going to the refugee camp in case he tried to stop her, but she didn't know what else to say.

"Why?" He repeated. "Why are you going to Lansing?"

"I'm alone. My family is gone and I need protection." She paused. "I need protection, food, and shelter, and I heard there's a refugee camp near Lansing."

The soldier looked directly at her unblinking. "Why don't you join the revolution? The camp is run by the government. They're dogs. Do you believe in them or in freedom from discrimination and repression?"

"I don't believe in anything. I just want protection, food, and shelter. The revolution seems volatile and the camp sounds stable. That's all." Emily looked at the ground.

"Stable? Ha!" The soldier's chuckle was dark, heavy. "If you think it's stable living in shitty conditions, and then being forced to move when the government decides they want the land you're living on to build a Cineplex or a mini-mall, you're an idiot. You'll get to that camp and they'll assign you some tent, and then they'll move you around, probably pass you around; the governor, his council, and that leech of his – Attorney General John Caring."

At this Emily's eyes darted back up to meet the soldier's. She was seething. Her father was not a rapist, not a leech, and not some government dog. "They wouldn't do that." She spat through her teeth.

"You bet your sweet ass they would. You know the problem with girls like you? You think life is all perfect because that's all you know. You don't know how the other half lives and you don't care. You don't see the government, in the middle of the night, moving homeless people from outside city limits into the city so the population goes up for the next census and the government can get more federal money. Do they provide housing for these people? Psychiatric help? Even food or water? No. They drop them off on the street, in bad neighborhoods where no one comes looking. Then they use that federal money to build more museums and parks to draw in tourists, and then when the tourists come they bus the homeless people back outside the city and claim that since they're not within city limits, they're not their responsibility."

Emily was speechless. She had no idea this happened. When she had volunteered at a soup kitchen once in high school, her father had explained that it was the job of private charities to take care of the homeless and public money went into trash clean up, the fire department, and the police. Maybe it wasn't true? Or maybe the soldier was lying?

"How do you know that?" she asked.

"How do I know? I know because I lived in one of those "bad neighborhoods" and I saw them drop off the homeless in buses and drive away. That was before they told me and my family that we had to be out of our apartment by December 31st. Why? Because they were bulldozing our apartment complex to build a new swimming pool for this summer's tourists. They offered us a check for one month's rent to 'help us with the transition to a new, better home.' Selfish bastards."

"Couldn't you just say no?" as she said it, Emily realized how naïve it sounded.

"Sure. I could say no, but then what? The government built the complex, they own it. I say no and I have no place to stay and no check. So, princess, what should I have done?"

Emily didn't reply.

"That's what I thought. What I did was take a stand. What I did was say 'no more of this bullshit.' I did my mandatory year of military service for this government, and now I'm going to take those skills they taught me and fight back."

They stood in silence for several minutes. The tension made the air thick. The soldier was looking above her head again and Emily was staring at the floor. He was right. She knew the neighborhoods he was talking about and she had never been there. Her parents had told her they were too dangerous and that if she wanted to help she could volunteer, so she had — at a soup kitchen at the church near her high school, but it smelled putrid and the people she served scared her with their missing teeth and overgrown hair, so she hadn't gone back. Now here she was, Emily Caring — tired, dirty, and homeless.

"I'm sorry." Emily said softly. She was crying.

"Oh hell." The soldier leaned down so he was closer to Emily's eye level. He rested his hand on her left shoulder, she flinched and he removed it. "How old are you? Nineteen? Twenty?"

"Twenty." She lifted her head up but her vision was clouded with tears.

The soldier nodded. "I have a daughter around your age. I wish she hadn't seen the things she has, and hadn't had the childhood she did, but I know none of that's her fault."

Emily gulped back a sob and wiped her nose with the back of her sleeve.

He went on, "It's not all your fault, you know. That you don't know how the world works."

She looked up now and met his eyes. He wasn't some drone either.

31

He was a father, trying his best to provide for his family.

"Now you listen, I was sent to make sure this town was clear of civilians. We're going to be planting land mines here tomorrow. I think you should join us, join the revolution, but for now you can go on to Lansing. I won't stop you."

Emily nodded. Not knowing what else to do.

"Take care of yourself, be careful." The soldier said as he stood aside to let Emily pass.

Emily knelt down to get her knapsack, and swung it over her shoulder as she stood back up. She kept her head down but whispered "thank you" as she walked past the soldier, then made her way down the stairs, out of the house and onto the street.

She traveled through the rest of night and into the next day, stopping briefly to eat and rest. She tried not to think about the soldier's story, only focusing on her goal. Once she made it to the camp she would take time to reflect, or not, she wasn't sure how much more disappointment she could handle. Her fourth night on the road, she made it there.

The Camp

It was twilight when she first saw the refugee camp. As she approached it, she gasped. She could see it from almost a mile away. It was an old baseball stadium that had been converted and repurposed. Giant spotlights were shining on all sides of it. There were tents spilling out from the side entrances, widening its boundaries. The perimeter was lined with tanks, and there was a single file line of refugees waiting to pass through a narrow space at the front entrance. Government soldiers were on either side of the line, keeping watch. They were eyeing the refugees and the roads from which they were entering.

Emily took her place at the end of the line. The woman in front of her had a baby strapped to her back. The baby was sleeping, drool hanging precariously from its lip. Emily watched the baby as the line moved; its chest rising and falling, deeply breathing as it slept. The line moved rather quickly. It only took her ten minutes to reach the front. The guard was holding a tablet.

"Name?"

Emily wasn't sure what name to give. Would it better at this moment to be John Caring's daughter or worse? This was a government run camp.

"Caring. Emily Caring."

The guard looked up. "Who is your father?"

Emily took a deep breath, "John Caring."

The guard straightened up. He scrolled with his finger on the tablet, his eyes scanning the screen. He paused, and then his index finger tapped the screen twice. "Come with me please. Leave your belongings here. They will be examined and returned to you." They walked through the metal detectors at the entrance together. As they entered the baseball stadium, Emily saw there were different groups of tents, and dirt paths separating them. The guard led her to a section in the far left of the outfield.

"All family members of government officials are given a private tent."

Emily almost screamed, "Is anyone else from my family here?"

"No. Oh no, I'm sorry to mislead you. You are the only one from Attorney General Caring's family in this camp."

Her face fell.

The guard took notice and added, "This is one of a few camps though. I'm sure they're fine."

The tent he took her to was rather large for one person. There was a cot and a space heater plugged into a cord coming from under the tent. They must be plugged into the electrical grid of the stadium, Emily thought. It was smart, using the stadium. It was wired for massive uses of electricity and could hold thousands of people. She sat down on the cot. She had made it here. She was safe and protected. Maybe that was what home meant? Emily took a deep breath and let the relief wash over her.

After several months, the camp morphed into a village. There was a section of medical tents, and a school was built. Some people had brought books with them and they organized a lending library. Tents were rearranged so one area off of a side entrance became a park. Eventually, Emily started working as a teacher at the elementary school; she liked being around children and it gave her a purpose. The grades weren't traditionally organized, since there weren't enough children to fill each class, but all the main disciplines were taught. Emily taught an English class of children ages eight to ten. She made a few friends, most were former university students like herself.

New refugees arrived at the camp almost daily in the first few months but no members of her family materialized. She stopped waiting for them after the first year. Sometimes she would lay awake at night thinking about what the soldier in Mason had said. Had her father known all that was happening? Had her mother? What else had been kept from her? It was painful for her to think of her father as anyone other than the man she knew him to be. Her memory of him was so clear and strong. She was afraid to let any damaging stories into her psyche for fear they would break her spirit, but she knew that one day, after the war, she would learn the truth. She resigned herself to living a quiet life, a teacher in a refugee camp with her own tent, waiting for the war to be over.

The war dragged on for four years and when it ended in 2060, Emily was told she had a month to leave the camp before it was closed. Before she could leave, however, it was required that she register in the New Republic. A soldier offered to drive her to the registration office. She was still John Caring's daughter, after all. Emily chose to walk, like the rest of the refugees who were not the progeny of former government officials. The registration office was about an hour outside Lansing in East Lansing. She left the next day at sunrise.

Present Day

She was staring at the gate. It was made of iron. Her breathing was shallow.

Emily could see where it had been welded together. The arches at the top were welded to tall poles, which were secured to the ground with cement. The registration office, just beyond the gate, was far less industrial. It had been hastily built. It was white, the walls were made of plaster, and the blue masking tape around the window frames had not yet been removed.

Over the past four years, she had imagined countless times how she would be reunited with her family, and all the scenarios had included the reunion itself – joyful embraces, tears, and an overwhelming sense of relief. She had not imagined the registration process, and now that she was here it was daunting.

"Even if their names aren't on that list, it doesn't mean they're not alive, it just means they haven't registered yet." She said quietly to herself. She had prepared herself for the worst, but as she walked forward she chose positive thinking. It was the only thing that could propel her through the gate and into the registration office.

She reached the office door and turned the brass doorknob. The office was one moderately-sized room; the size of one of the lecture halls at her old university. The walls were white and it smelled of fresh paint. In the middle of the room there was a desk, and behind that a wall with large sheets of paper tacked to it. There was a small, bespectacled man behind the desk. He looked to be in his early thirties, thin, with gelled brown hair that was parted down the middle.

She approached the desk.

The man glanced up from the tablet he was typing on. "Name?"

She took a deep breath, pausing to steady herself. "Caring. Emily Caring."

"Date of birth?"

"June 2, 2035."

"And from which former state do you originate?"

"Michigan."

He handed her the tablet. "Please verify that your name is spelled correctly, and then fill in your current mailing address, phone number, and e-mail address."

Emily typed carefully until the form was complete. She looked it over, making sure everything was correct, and then handed the tablet back to him.

"Okay, now who do you want on your contacts list?"

"Excuse me?"

"Your contacts list. If someone sees your name up there and wants to contact you we can't give them your information unless they're on your contacts list."

"Oh, I'm sorry. Yes, of course." Emily hadn't known about the "contacts list" but she quickly listed her family members as the man typed.

The printer at his feet spat out an index card with a barcode.

"Here is your registration card. You can present this when you return to the camp as proof of registration. That barcode is the way you will be identified. It will be scanned at every check point in the New Republic. If it is lost or damaged, you must return here for a new card."

Emily took the card, nodding. She tucked it in her pocket.

"Okay you're the first one to register today so the list behind me is up to date." He turned around in his chair and pointed to the back wall. "The list is alphabetical by surname, starting with the list on your left. Everyone who has registered will be up there. If you see a friend or family member you wish to contact, come back here and if you're on their contacts list, I can give you their information."

Emily walked to the wall of names. Her heart was pounding. She could feel it in her chest, in her ears. Her breathing was even only because she was counting each breath to keep herself calm.

She stood in front of the first list and scanned the surnames. The last surname on it was "Browning." She moved to the second list. "Buckley," "Cane." She stopped.

Caring, Catherine

Caring, Wallace

Annabelle's Story

Four Years Ago

She twisted and tossed in her sleeping bag, asleep but vividly dreaming.

"Annabelle!" Her brother, Christopher, shook her awake. "Annabelle, get up. We have to go. The rebels are moving east."

Annabelle and Christopher were four years apart, but looked identical. Both had dark blonde hair, and almond-shaped brown eyes. Annabelle was an economics major at Columbia University in New York, while Christopher wasn't sure what he wanted to do. The revolution had changed him though; it had given him a purpose. He needed to keep them alive and protect Annabelle.

Annabelle blinked several times as she awoke and realized where she was. She had been having another nightmare. She was trying to run from the rebels but her feet were too heavy. She willed them to move but they wouldn't. The rebels were gaining on her and she was paralyzed. As she climbed out of her sleeping bag she shook her legs out, relieved the nightmare was over.

The rebels had come for her family nearly a month ago. She was the only one home that night. Christopher had pulled into the driveway as they were taking her to their truck. He had seen two soldiers holding her arms behind her back. As he stepped out of his car, one soldier pulled out a gun and pointed it at him.

"We're here with the revolution. Put your hands up, where we can see them."

Without hesitating, Christopher pulled a gun from his waistband and shot that soldier in the neck. The second soldier dropped his hold of Annabelle's arm, and as he raised his gun Christopher shot him in the neck too. Both men lay crumpled on the ground, by the purple hydrangeas their mother had planted. Annabelle froze. Everything had happened so fast. Christopher was her younger brother and with her away at university, she wasn't sure if she even knew him anymore. As she became more conscious of the situation, he was already entering the house.

"Come on," he beckoned to her. "We don't have very much time before someone realizes they're missing, we need to get supplies."

She followed him into the house, through the living room to the kitchen. Christopher immediately emptied his backpack onto the counter, arranging everything within view. He had books, weapons, and a water bottle. Then he started emptying the cabinets of non-perishables and putting them on the kitchen table. After he was finished with that, he began repacking his backpack with various items: a pocket knife, baked beans, granola bars, and a lighter. He was quick but methodical. Annabelle just watched him, mesmerized.

"Who are you?"

"What?"

"How did you know how to do that?" she asked and then gestured toward the cabinets. "And this?"

He paused, glancing back at her. "I'm in training, it's my mandatory year. You know that."

"Yes, but I didn't realize you actually knew how to shoot people. Or that you carried weapons."

"What did you think we were doing?"

"I don't know. Not that. More Boy Scout stuff, like pitching a tent or building a fire."

"Well we do that too." Then he paused, looking at Annabelle's dumbfounded expression. "Didn't the guys in your class tell you anything about training?"

"No, I mean they mentioned it, but they never talked about it like it was serious. Not like when dad did his year. We don't go to war anymore. We're a peaceful country now."

Christopher kept packing. "Yeah, well. Maybe that was true four years ago but not for my class. Things are more serious now, with the rebellion building. We've done shooting drills, hand to hand combat. I have a permit to carry a firearm, loaded with tranquilizers, to and from class. Thankfully, I had class tonight. Who knows what would have happened?" He zipped his backpack, then shifted his weight and hoisted it onto his back, "Okay, let's go."

"Where?"

"We'll find somewhere to hide until we can make it to a refugee camp or out of the country. Either way, we can't stay here. They told us in training that something like this might happen if the revolution got going. The rebels came here for us, and two of their soldiers are out cold on our front lawn. We can't stay here. We have to go, now."

Annabelle followed him out of the house and onto the street. The soldiers were still lying there. She turned away as they walked across the lawn.

"If we cut through the forest preserve we'll have cover, at least for a while. Then I'm thinking we should head to Lansing or maybe Ann Arbor?"

Annabelle nodded, "Sure, Ann Arbor sounds good. We certainly know how to get there."

They started on their journey, heading first to Ann Arbor and then Lansing. There were refugee camps in both cities but they were turned away due to overcrowding. Michigan had four camps, but the others were up north and more difficult to reach.

After that, they stayed in two homes that were part of The Network, a group of people who were not a threat to the revolution. They secretly allowed families of government officials into their homes for a couple of nights at a time. They had learned about The Network after they were turned away in Lansing. A young woman in line ahead of them was talking to one of the guards, discussing other options for survival. Her husband worked in the governor's office. He'd been taken but she had escaped. She was desperate for protection. They watched as the guard scribbled down a name and address on a piece of paper. When he saw them looking, they turned away, afraid.

"Don't worry," he said. "I can help."

He explained that The Network was similar to the Underground Railroad during the antebellum period, but instead of evading capture by former slave owners, people evaded the revolutionaries. And like many of those who used the Underground Railroad, the goal was to make it to Canada.

Annabelle hoped that once they got to Canada she would be able to finally turn on her phone and call her parents. Her phone was solar powered, but a woman in The Network said the rebels had taken over the government monitoring system and were tracking all unaccounted government personnel and their families via the GPS in their phones.

Their parents, Michael and Isabelle Stevenson, both worked for the government. They were midlevel officers in the Environmental Safety office. Nothing glamorous or exciting, but their positions had made all of them targets. They had met in graduate school in Ann Arbor. They chose to move to Detroit because of their commitment to the environment which was being compromised by the automotive industry, and also because it was close to camping and the great outdoors.

They had moved when Detroit was at its worst, after the 2025 riots, and had stayed out of a sense of duty to the city and its people. After many years of government service and carefully saved vacation days, they had decided to travel in Italy for two weeks. Christopher was old enough to be home alone, and Annabelle would be home on spring break just in case. They knew they could trust her to keep him in line. They had no idea that the rebellion would spread so fast and endanger their family.

Annabelle was very smart but academic. She didn't have any military training or survival skills. Christopher had less direction. He liked to read, he liked his combat training, he liked playing basketball with his friends, and he had a crush on a boy in his statistics class named Greg. That was about it. He didn't like thinking about the future or about adulthood. The war had changed all that. Now, he was planning their route to safety.

They had to circle back to Detroit to cross the border, and that was rebel-held territory. They had survived thanks to The Network but he didn't know what to expect at the border. It was hard to tell what was happening in a war you were constantly hiding from.

"How much further until the next stop?" Annabelle asked.

Christopher looked over his shoulder at her. He remembered a time when she had towered over him. He had been four and small for his age, and she was eight. They had been at the park. He had gotten in a fight with another boy his age over who was next in line for the slide and the boy pushed him out of the way. Christopher had fallen on the ground. Annabelle had seen what happened. She marched over, picked the other boy up and out of the line entirely. Picked Christopher up, brushed the dirt off of his chest and said to the line of preschoolers, "It is Christopher's turn. You will all get your turn but you have to wait in line... patiently." He had looked up at her and felt so protected and proud. Now she was almost a foot shorter than he was.

"I'm not sure. There's one more stop on The Network before Detroit but I don't know if we should stop there. The closer we get to rebel-held territory, the more likely that we'll be caught."

He paused. He had said it so resolutely, but he wasn't actually sure if he was right. He was used to Annabelle expressing her opinion, and telling him what to do. Since he had shot the soldiers she had been mostly silent, relying on his opinion. The role reversal made him uneasy.

"What do you think?" he added.

Annabelle looked away. On some level she had known the revolution was coming. The skewed economic policies in Detroit had created such profound inequality it was only a matter of time before there was a revolt. The rebuilding of Detroit had been done poorly, by ambitious, greedy men who wanted glory at the expense of those they had deemed too poor to fight back. Well they had been wrong and now her family was paying the price.

She paused, pulling her hair up into a high bun. Once her hair was secure, she turned to face him.

"I don't think we should trust anyone."

Christopher was confused. What did she mean? "Well, we trusted the people in The Network so far and that's turned out fine. Do you think that was a mistake?"

"No, not exactly, but it could turn out to be. I'm just worried that if The Network can tell us where to go and who to trust, it could also be turned against us. Think about it, they have the names and faces of everyone on the run. That information could be very valuable to the revolution."

"But don't you think if they wanted to turn us in they would have?"

"If they're playing the short game, sure, but not if they're playing the long game."

"Why didn't you say anything? Speak up?"

Annabelle paused, "I wasn't sure if I should. I don't have any experience with this, with war. And when it came down to it I was just going to go with those soldiers. I didn't resist. It never occurred to me that they would hurt me, but you just knew. You didn't hesitate, you took action. I'd never seen that before."

"I don't have any experience with war either, but I've been doing all this training and I don't know, I think it's just something I'm good at."

The two stood in silence. It was an odd moment for both of them. They were alone, relying only on each other. They didn't know where their parents, grandparents, or friends were. They didn't know who was still alive or who had been killed. For all they knew, they were all that was left of their family.

Annabelle spoke first, "Okay, from now on let's communicate better. Make decisions together. I'll speak up more, I promise."

Christopher nodded, and they both started walking toward Detroit. They spent the next two days on the road until they reached Ambassador Bridge, the bridge from Detroit to Windsor, Ontario, Canada.

————

The bridge stood out on the horizon. It was the first time they had seen it empty, not a vehicle in sight. Usually there were commercial trucks taking supplies across the border. The bridge was made of pale green metal; it reminded Christopher of the Statue of Liberty in a way it hadn't before. He eyed the shoreline of the Detroit River over which the bridge presided. It had once been the longest suspension bridge in the world, unseated by the George Washington Bridge in the 1930s. A large flag for the revolution had been hoisted up to the top left spire on the American side of the bridge. The flag was white with two large, horizontal red stripes on the top and bottom borders. In the center of the flag was an eagle, its talons empty; underneath the eagle in black script was the word *libertatem*, Latin for "freedom." There were a dozen or so soldiers milling about by the entrance to the bridge. The checkpoint structure was still intact but there was a tank next to it now. The tank had *libertatem* spray painted in black on its left side.

Annabelle and Christopher sat crouched several hundred feet away from the bridge, in the top floor of an abandoned warehouse in Riverside Park which borders the Detroit River. Most of the city was abandoned, even more so than at the turn of the century when the city had experienced the collapse of the automotive industry and the resulting economic decline.

"So how do you think we should cross?" Annabelle asked.

"I don't think we can, not directly anyway."

"Do you think we'll have to swim?"

"Maybe, it's what, twenty-five or thirty miles long? And I don't think the currents will be too bad. I doubt there are any shipments coming through by tanker anymore, but I'm not sure."

"Thirty miles? That's really far. I'm not sure if I can make it."

"Sure you can, you've heard about all those drunks and frat guys doing it on a dare. You're in way better shape than them. You can totally do it." Christopher paused, waiting for Annabelle to say something. Silence. "Annabelle?"

"I'm thinking." Annabelle pulled her knees up to her chest and peered out of the sliver of window pane. "How much food do we have left? How many days can we last?"

"Three, maybe four days if we ration."

"But we'll need plenty of energy to swim across if it comes to that so let's say three days. I think we should stay here, observe them for the next two days and then make a decision. We've made it this far. We need to be strategic."

"But what if the war escalates in that time? What if there's more border control?"

"There's no way to know which way the war is going unless we watch. We've spent the last month hiding from it. Let's watch it play out here, at the border, for a couple days. I think we'll see enough to know if it's safe to cross."

Christopher nodded, "Okay."

And so they waited, and watched.

————

Annabelle peered through the window pane as a truck pulled up to the border checkpoint. It was the most action she had seen at the border in the past two days. "Christopher, come here, something's happening."

Christopher got up from where he had been sitting, reading *Franny and Zooey* by J.D. Salinger. He had ventured out once since they had gotten back to Detroit to try and find food. He had managed to enter three abandoned houses, and had come out with a can of baked beans and the book. It was his mother's favorite book but he had never read it, until now.

"What? What's going on?"

Nothing much had happened yesterday or this morning; a few soldiers had changed their positions. It didn't seem very organized though. The shifts were not exact and for the most part the soldiers just looked bored. A soldier got out of the passenger seat of the truck and strode to the back of the vehicle looking very proud. He pulled the bolt up and out of the hinge and then opened the back doors. Three men in dusty, worn, business suits shuffled out slowly, one-by-one. Annabelle gasped.

"What? Who are they?" Christopher asked.

"It's Mr. Caring, Emily Caring's dad. Remember her? We were friends in grade school. I think her brother, Daniel, is in your grade. And that's, well I think that's the Governor, George Adams. I don't know who the third man is though."

Christopher leaned in closer to the window pane, "What are they doing with them?"

"I don't know."

The soldier who had been in the driver's seat got out of the truck and raised his gun toward the prisoners, while the first soldier ran to the checkpoint office. The prisoners did not move though they looked as if they were about to faint. Their faces were pale and their suits looked a size too big, hanging off their bony shoulders. Their hands were behind their backs, handcuffed.

The first soldier emerged from the check point office with another soldier and both men walked toward the prisoners. Then, a black Lincoln Town Car pulled up slowly next to the truck.

"What is that? I mean, who is in that car?" Christopher asked.

Annabelle didn't reply. The question was rhetorical. She held her breath, waiting to see who would come out of the car. With all the lengths they had gone to hiding from the revolution, it had never occurred to her to question who was leading it. She had considered it a grass roots movement of society's forgotten, mob mentality run amok. For there to be one leader would be counterintuitive to their cause, wouldn't it?

The car slowed down to a stop. The driver, in civilian clothes, got out and went around to the side of the car to open the door. As he approached, the door opened from the inside and a small, be-spectacled man got out. He was wearing all black. His top was a thigh-length tunic which was buttoned up to the collar. His trousers were slightly too short, brushing the tops of his black, patent leather shoes. He had jet black hair in a crew cut. His race was unclear but as he turned to survey the prisoners it occurred to Annabelle that he might be of Asian descent, partially anyway. Everyone in the U.S. was such an ethnic mix that someone with one racial heritage was rare.

She couldn't hear what he was saying but she could tell he was speaking loudly and saying something important from the facial reactions of the soldiers. He was gesticulating and his chest was puffed up. Finally, after ten minutes or so of this, he crossed his arms over his chest and stood silently. The soldiers hurried to gather their guns, and then each knelt before him holding out a weapon. He surveyed the options.

"You don't think he's going to kill someone do you?" Christopher whispered.

Annabelle paused and said, "I don't know." But she did know. Her chest felt heavy and her stomach was in knots. She had premonitions sometimes, feelings about the future that swept over her in waves. She was having one now. The leader of the revolution, if that's who he was, was going to shoot someone and that person was going to die.

The leader picked up a handgun from the soldier to his immediate left. The soldiers then stood up and two of them went to the prisoners, positioning them further apart from one another and in a straight line facing the leader. The leader held the gun while speaking and gesturing. John Caring grimaced, while the Governor and the other man stood still, eyes closed. Then the leader, without pausing, fired two shots into the Governor's chest.

Annabelle and Christopher gasped.

The Governor's body crumpled to the ground. John Caring and the other man knelt down next to him. The leader looked away and then handed the gun to his driver, who passed it to a nearby soldier. The leader raised his hand in the air, waving to the soldiers as he and the driver returned to the car. The soldiers waited until the car had driven away before they pulled John Caring and the other man up from the ground and marched them back to the truck. Annabelle and Christopher looked on silently as two of the soldiers tied large rocks to the Governor's ankles, and tossed his lifeless body into the Detroit River. In the background, the truck drove slowly away from border.

That evening, Annabelle and Christopher decided they would swim across the Detroit River to Canada.

———

It was pitch black. Most of the soldiers were in the checkpoint building. One was standing outside with a rifle slung over his shoulder, a night stick in his belt, and a flashlight he used to sweep the shoreline occasionally. Christopher had been on watch the previous night and noted the guard change times. It was almost 2 am, a new guard would be coming out soon and during the change there would be at least two minutes when no one was monitoring the shoreline; plenty of time for them to slip into the water and get far enough across the river not to be detected.

"Do you have everything?" Annabelle asked.

"Yes."

"And you burned the books and our bags. There can't be any trace of us."

"Yes, in the trash can in the back while you were sleeping. The fire was very low. No one saw me."

Annabelle smiled and said softly, "Okay."

Their phones were waterproof but even so they wrapped them in plastic bags and stored them in their pants' pockets. That was it.

Those were the only possessions they were bringing. Everything else they had left behind at their house or destroyed.

As they approached the water, their breathing shallow and their steps light, they looked out toward Ontario. They didn't know what would happen when they got to Canada. They didn't have any friends or relatives there. What if the Canadian government denied them asylum? They had to take the chance. It was their only feasible option for survival.

———

As the guards changed, they slowly approached the water. Annabelle braced herself for how cold it would be. Christopher waded in first, he glanced back and she followed. The water was freezing and her legs began to prickle. Christopher dove under and began swimming freestyle stroke; she did the same but he was much faster. Every time she looked up, he was further and further ahead of her. She wanted to cry out, say something to get his attention but she didn't want to draw any attention to them. Her chest was aching. Why didn't women get military training too? She thought she had "lucked out," but now she desperately wished the old patriarchal standards had been dropped and that women were made to train and serve the mandatory year. She had little physical endurance and no formal training in long distance swimming. She looked up again at the lights of Ontario reflecting on the water. The night sky was clear and filled with stars. Christopher was waiting just ahead, treading water. He had stopped when he saw how far behind she was. She felt momentary relief and then heard a booming voice coming from on top of the bridge. All of a sudden, spotlights were circling them.

"You are making an illegal crossing. Stop. I repeat. You are making an illegal crossing. If you do not stop immediately, we will have no choice but to stop you."

They were caught. Christopher looked to Annabelle, his eyes pleading. She was his older sister; she was supposed to take care of him. She summoned all her resolve and nodded at him. Without hesitating he plunged deep below the surface, she inhaled sharply and dove down as well, swimming with all her might. She heard muffled gunfire and felt small waves darting past her, caused by bullets entering the water. She couldn't see Christopher and she wasn't even sure if she was swimming in a straight line but she kept going, coming up for air quickly and then diving back down. The spotlights were trailing them and she could hear indecipherable words booming above them. Nearly twenty minutes passed. She was getting tired.

When she came back up for air a final time the spotlights were gone and instead she saw a bright light shining from the shoreline. Her chest was heaving and she dove back down, willing herself forward, pushing ahead. Her head was throbbing with pain and she was feeling dizzy. She needed air but she didn't want to risk coming up again. She pushed herself forward, struggling with each stroke. Then she felt a hand grab her wrist. She shook it off, panicked. It grabbed hold of her again. She didn't think she had any strength left but at the thought of apprehension she started thrashing in the water, desperately trying to reach the surface. As she reached up, her hands clawing at the water around her, the hand grabbed her wrist firmly and pulled her toward the surface. She started to black out. The last thing she remembered was seeing someone in scuba gear with a red maple leaf on their chest.

"Annabelle Stevenson, age twenty-one. She's one of the refugees from the New Republic."

Annabelle's eyes slowly opened and the room came into focus—white, chalky walls and an IV drip hanging next to her. She was in a hospital bed surrounded by young men and women, presumably doctors, in white lab coats. They were all staring at her, holding clipboards.

"Hello?" her voice was gravely, she felt groggy. Her mouth felt like it was filled with cotton balls. She cleared her throat, "Hello? Where is Christopher Stevenson, my brother?"

One of the doctors, an older woman, the one who had said her name, came toward her, "Hi, Annabelle, I'm Dr. Patel. You're in Windsor Regional Hospital. You were rescued by the Coast Guard and brought here for your recovery."

"But where is my brother?"

"Your brother?"

"Yes." Annabelle sat up then, gripped with fear. "My brother. Christopher Stevenson. He's seventeen years old. Is he here?"

Dr. Patel's brow furrowed as she flipped through the pages on her clipboard, "I don't see another Stevenson on the patient list."

Annabelle's mind began racing. Had he been captured on the American side of the border? Had he been shot? Was she the only one who had been rescued? Just then she heard the door open and close and Christopher walked in, carrying a tray of food.

"Oh, so you're up." He smiled at her as he made his way around the doctors standing in the room. He placed the tray on a table in the corner and when he got to her bedside she was crying.

"Hey, come on. It's okay. Annabelle, it's okay. We're safe now. You were only out for a couple of hours. It's still Tuesday for crying out loud. We're fine."

Annabelle looked up, "It's only Tuesday? We left Detroit this morning and now we're here, in Canada?"

Christopher nodded.

Then she started laughing. She didn't know why but the joy and relief erupted out of her and she was laughing and crying at the same time.

Dr. Patel turned around and ushered the younger doctors out of the room, "This must be the brother. Okay everyone, let's give the patient some room. We'll come back and you can evaluate her and do your presentations later."

The door closed behind them and Christopher went to the table, sat down in the adjacent chair and started eating his sandwich.

"So what happened? Did they just give us asylum?" Annabelle asked.

Christopher chewed slowly, then paused. "Yes, as far as I can tell the Canadians are taking everyone who can make it across the border, so far. They said they would process us in a few days, but they brought us here for you to recover... no questions asked. Apparently we're not the first ones to attempt the Detroit River crossing, and from what the Coast Guard said they've been getting refugees all over Canada."

Annabelle nodded. "What about mom and dad? Were you able to call them?"

"I called their hotel but they checked out when they were supposed to, last month. I asked the guy from the hotel if he knew of any Americans being taken or staying in other hotels. He wasn't very helpful. They could be fine though."

"What about our phones? When we got here did you turn them on? They might have sent us a message?"

"They're gone. They must have fallen out of our pockets when we were swimming."

Annabelle didn't know what to feel. She was relieved that they had made it here, but frustrated that they couldn't locate their parents. Then she realized one thing she was definitely feeling, hunger. "Can I have the other half of your sandwich?"

"Oh yeah, sorry, of course."

Christopher brought the tray over and set it on her lap. He sat at the end of her bed as they ate. She looked out the window at the city of Windsor, Ontario. They were American refugees, alone in a foreign country, with no idea what would happen next, but at least for now they knew they were safe.

Ben's Story

Four years ago

The Interview

"So what can you contribute here that another candidate can't? What sets you apart?"

Ben was in the last few minutes of his final interview. He had interviewed at five different companies that were hiring engineers. All were more or less the same.

"I think that I bring a unique perspective as an engineer who was trained on foreign machinery." Ben leaned back slightly but maintained eye contact with the interviewer. "For example, I understand reverse flow systems, using both the American and European models, and though I wouldn't be working with European models here, I am able to trouble-shoot and problem-solve using a much richer knowledge base than an engineer who only knows American systems."

"Very good, very good. Do you have any questions?"

"No, I think you covered everything."

The interviewer nodded, "Well, Mr. Hughes it was a pleasure speaking with you. You certainly are a qualified candidate and we will be in touch."

The man rose and Ben did too. They shook hands and Ben left the conference room. As he reached the elevator he saw another young man, dressed in a similar suit to the one he was wearing, being called into the conference room. Over three hundred people had applied to this position and it was the same everywhere; too many candidates, not enough jobs.

Ben took the elevator down to the lobby. He had some time before he needed to be at the bus station. Maybe he would stop and get a coffee. He pushed the revolving door to exit and he had only taken two steps onto the sidewalk when he was blown backwards against the side of the building. His head hit the brick wall hard and he stumbled forward. His ears were ringing and his vision was blurry. He stumbled again and landed on his knees. People were running past him and there was smoke in the air. Dust was swirling around him. He tried to stand up but he was dizzy. Slowly he crawled around the corner into an alley and sat up, leaning his back against the wall of the building. He took several deep breaths as he tried to get his bearings. He heard sirens in the distance and a woman was screaming. What was happening? Then he heard gunfire.

His parents had warned him about the rebellion that was building in Michigan. "It only takes one bullet to turn a peaceful protest into a battle," his father had said. The rebels had been protesting for months though and nothing had changed. Ben was an American citizen and his only family stateside was in the Midwest, on the Indiana/Michigan border. It made sense to interview there. It was the only "home" in this country he had ever known.

People were running past the alley and Ben wasn't sure what to do. He wasn't sure if he could walk, or even stand. So he crawled further into the alley and hid behind a dumpster. The gunfire grew louder and he heard rhythmic chanting. At first the words were unclear but as his head cleared and his ears stopped ringing, he understood what they were saying.

"Freedom from fear!"

"Give back our rights!"

"No more chains, we're the New Republic!"

He looked down the alleyway and saw marchers in the street; a few held guns and they were firing them into the air. At least they weren't firing them at people, as far as he could tell. Ben waited several minutes until the marchers had passed and then slowly stood up. He was feeling better, almost back to normal. He decided to change out of his suit. From what he remembered hearing on the news, the rebels were protesting the government and government officials. Hopefully in street clothes he wouldn't be a target.

He had traveled on the bus in jeans and a sweatshirt, carrying his suit in a garment bag so as not to wrinkle it. He moved further behind the dumpster and pulled the clothes from his backpack. What should he do with his suit? After he changed, he threw the suit and the garment bag in the dumpster.

He swung his backpack over his shoulders and made his way down the alley and out onto the street. People were walking slowly, looking dazed. He didn't know what was going on but he needed to get out of the city and back to his cousins' house. He headed to the Southfield Greyhound Bus Station. He wasn't sure the extent of the damage but maybe someone at the bus station would know. In the first block he saw burn marks on the sidewalk where two public garbage cans had been. That must have been the explosion. There was still smoke in the distance.

As he walked up Twelve Mile Road, his eyes scanned ahead looking for signs of the revolution. Had there been a larger explosion? Everything seemed so calm. When he reached Lahser Road he turned to head to the bus station and saw smoke several blocks away. As he got closer he realized what had happened – they had blown up the bus station. Systematically destroy the infrastructure – a basic warfare technique. Ben sighed.

Outside Detroit, the transportation system in Michigan, and most of the rural Midwestern states, consisted of buses and personal vehicles. The latter of which was limited to one per family due to emissions restrictions passed by the previous administration. He wasn't sure what to do next. On the one hand, he could call his cousins and see if they could come pick him up. It was several hours away but his options were limited. On the other hand, if the revolution was getting more serious, which it seemed to be, then the rebels might already be tapping phone lines. The less he exposed himself to surveillance, the better. He shook his head. No, it couldn't be that serious. He took out his phone and called his uncle. He answered, and Ben explained what had happened.

"We saw it on the news. We've been trying to call you. Didn't you get our messages?"

Ben didn't have any missed calls or voicemails. He got a sick feeling in the pit of his stomach.

The rebels had hacked into the phone system. They were probably listening right now.

"Yeah... yeah I got them. I'm just going to catch the bus back. Don't worry."

"But I thought you said there was no bus. They blew up the station didn't they? Ben?"

He hung up the phone and turned it off.

Ben had grown up in Beirut, Lebanon, the son of an American diplomat. He could recognize the sounds of bombs and bullets, and differentiate them from fireworks and car backfires. His family's phone lines had been tapped by everyone, including the U.S. government – especially the U.S. government. As an American citizen born in Michigan, he had returned to serve his mandatory year before attending the American University of Beirut for college, then the American University of Cairo for graduate school. The social and economic inequality in the U.S. hadn't affected him. He knew about the instituting of the mandatory military year, the 2025 riots, and the new federally enforced emissions standards.

Ben didn't know Michigan's geography though. He didn't know its surface streets or even its highways. He couldn't use the GPS on his phone since the rebels could be tracking him. He would need a map, a hard-copy, paper map. Where would he even get one? He thought for a minute. The library; there were still hard copies of books at the library. Everything else was digital.

A man was walking toward him. He was older, probably retired.

"Excuse me?"

He looked up when Ben addressed him. "Can I help you son?"

"Yes, I think so. I'm looking for the public library. Do you have one?

Is it near here?"

The man chuckled, "Yes, of course we have one. And it is near here, just a couple blocks away on Evergreen Road, in City Center Park. I'm not sure if it's open though. They cut back their hours years ago, and given all the commotion they might have closed for the day."

Ben nodded, "Thank you. And, I'm sorry but I'm not from around here. Where's Evergreen Road?"

The man smiled and when he lifted his arm to point, Ben saw the black band around his arm. He was part of the revolution, or a sympathizer anyway.

"It's just a couple blocks over, head down to Eleven Mile Road and take a left. You'll hit Evergreen within a couple blocks and then you'll see the park. You can't miss it. You're sure I can't help you with anything?"

"No, that's okay. Thank you." Ben quickly walked away without looking back. Once he got to the park, he was relieved to see the library's lights were on inside. It was much larger than he expected, with giant windows covering most of the front façade and wrapping around the sides. When he entered, however, it was instantly clear that the library didn't get much foot traffic. The atrium-style entry-way must have been grand in its day but the canary yellow paint was chipping, and other colors that once had been bright had been dulled by the sun. There was one librarian behind a desk marked "Information" who was tapping on a tablet.

"Hello, I'm looking for a map, or maps rather, of Michigan. Where can I find them?"

The librarian looked up, surprised. She had that vague look of eth-nic ambiguity. Part Asian, part African American, part Caucasian, maybe Hispanic – high cheekbones, large nose and thin eyes; she lifted her head up slowly to address him. "A map? You want a map from a book?"

"Yes, I do."

She gave him a skeptical look, like perhaps he was trying to trick her. When he didn't move, she sighed and stood up, "Follow me." She walked out from behind the desk and Ben followed her to a row of bookshelves near the back. A dusty sign that read "Geography" hung from the ceiling. "These haven't been updated since about 2030, but if you need any maps they'll be in here."

"And what if I need to copy them?"

"Excuse me?"

"Copy them, like make a paper copy. Is there a machine for that?"

The librarian looked confused, "Why can't you just scan it with your device?"

"I just want a paper copy. I know it's a little odd but I have bad eyes."

"Of course, yes, we have a printer. You can use my tablet to scan whatever you need and I'll print it for you."

"Great, thank you. I really appreciate it."

He spent the next hour going over old maps, finally settling on four that were the most comprehensive without being too detailed. The librarian scanned and printed them for him, and then he spent another hour plotting his route. It would take him several days, maybe a week, but he could get there on foot.

The Journey

It was already midday. He wouldn't get too far before nightfall. He had stopped by a grocery store on his way out of town and picked up some supplies: instant coffee and oatmeal, nuts and berries, and other non-perishables. He had also bought a camping stove from a hardware store. During his mandatory year it wasn't just military training but survival skills he had learned. Sometimes it seemed as if they were training for the apocalypse; the end of society as they knew it. It occurred to him now that maybe they had been.

He traveled on side streets until he hit Route 5. It was mostly farmland in this area. After the 2025 riots over food shortages, the Midwest had been dubbed the "agrarian sector" and towns had been bulldozed to make room for new farmland. Then, as the revolution spread, many of those farms had been abandoned as people fled to other parts of the country or abroad. Farming wasn't lucrative, government subsidies weren't enough, and people had to survive. As the sun was setting he saw an abandoned warehouse up ahead. He would spend the night there.

It was dark by the time he reached the warehouse. He slowly opened the door. Someone had been here or still was; he could sense it. He pulled the switchblade out of his pocket and concealed it in his sweatshirt. He had excelled in hand to hand combat during his mandatory year.

"Hello?" His voice echoed. There was a lofted room, probably an office, at the back of the warehouse and the door was ajar. "Hello?

Is anyone in here?"

"Who are you?" A female voice answered, it was blunt, severe.

Ben readied himself for an attack but tried to sound calm, jovial.

"Hello! Someone is here. I knew it. I have a sense for these things. Are you up there in the office?"

"You didn't answer my question. Who are you?"

"Oh yes, sorry. I'm Ben. Benjamin Hughes. The revolutionaries attacked the town I was in so..." He decided to lie about how long he'd been traveling. He didn't want this stranger to know where he was coming from, in case she was a revolutionary, "I've been on the road for a few days. I assume that's why you're hiding. Don't worry, I won't hurt you."

"How do you know I'm not a revolutionary? I'm armed."

"Okay sure. Yes. I suppose you could be a revolutionary but I'm telling you I'm not one. That makes me pretty vulnerable if you are one, so maybe give me the benefit of the doubt? Or not. I get that. I'm just trying to find somewhere to sleep tonight. I can stay down here and you can stay up there, or you can come down and introduce yourself."

He waited. Maybe there were more people here but he didn't think so. Eventually, she answered.

"All right. I'm coming down. Don't move and don't shine your flashlight in my face."

He watched the door to the office slowly open and a girl appeared.

She looked younger than her voice had indicated. Her head was down and she held her flashlight ahead of her. She was slim and she moved gracefully, cautiously. As she walked toward him she lifted her head and met his gaze. She was beautiful and it caught him off guard. Her eyes were lit up by the flashlight. They were green and piercing, almost luminescent. Her dark hair was pulled up into a high bun, but wisps of hair fell around her face and neck.

"I'm Emily, Emily Johnson."

He repeated the name in his head. Emily Johnson — such a plain name for a girl who clearly wasn't. He gathered himself, regaining what composure he had lost when he first saw her.

"Hi Emily Johnson, it's nice to meet you."

They exchanged pleasantries but it was clear she was wary of him. Eventually they said goodnight and she returned to the office. Ben lay down on the floor, using his backpack as a pillow. He thought about the long journey ahead and how much he wished he was already safe at his cousins' house. Maybe he never should have come here to interview. It was tough though, as a U.S. citizen trying to find work abroad; the visa restrictions and bureaucracy were daunting and the job prospects weren't that great anyway. And now here he was, in an abandoned warehouse, with a scared girl hiding in an office. He instinctively wanted to protect her, to take care of her, but he knew she wouldn't let him. So he put her out of his mind for the moment, closed his eyes and fell asleep.

In the morning he woke up with the sun. Emily was still asleep, or so he thought, unless she had slipped out during the night but he was pretty sure he would have heard. She would have walked past him.

He got out the camping stove and started boiling water to make oatmeal and coffee. It wasn't that bad, living like this. He just had to lay low and make it through the next few days.

"Good morning," her voice was softer than the night before.

He turned and saw her standing in the doorway to the office. The sun framed her silhouette.

"Morning, you sleep okay?"

"Yes, thank you. I did. You?"

"Yeah, I can pretty much sleep anywhere. I used to fall asleep in the car all the time as a kid." He chuckled again. "Want some breakfast? I've got coffee and oatmeal."

Emily nodded as she made her way down the stairs, "Sure, thanks. That's really nice of you."

"Of course, we revolutionaries have to stick together."

She froze.

"It was a joke, sorry. Man, you must have really been through something."

"Haven't you?"

Ben shrugged, "Not really. I was up north for a job interview. My parents live abroad, and the only family I have around here are my cousins. I was staying with them for a week to interview around here. You'd think more people would need to hire engineers with all the construction they're doing, but the competition is stiff. Anyway, they said there were going to be more peaceful protests but something was off. I'm telling you, I get a feeling about these things. Sure enough, within twenty-four hours all hell breaks loose and I end up on the road. My phone is dead now but I was able to call my parents and tell them I'm okay. I'll call them again when I get back to Elkhart. This country isn't what it used to be, that's for sure, but what do the revolutionaries want with me? I was born here, sure, but I didn't grow up here and my parents don't work for the government. Some job interview week. Man, I am never coming back here again."

He had woven a couple lies into his story, just to be safe.

Emily's face fell. She looked, in a word, defeated. She shifted uncomfortably and sat down next to the stove. Ben felt instantly guilty. Somehow, inadvertently, he had managed to hurt her feelings. He passed her some coffee and oatmeal. He didn't know what to say so he started telling jokes. Corny, simple jokes he had memorized as a kid. It cheered her up and soon they were both laughing.

After breakfast they parted ways. It didn't make sense for them to travel together. She was heading north and he was heading south. As he began walking something unexpected happened though – he missed her.

———

Ben estimated that it would take him four days to walk to Elkhart. Averaging ten hours a day. He could easily survive on the supplies he had gathered. The only variable was the rebels. He hadn't heard of any violence before the explosions in Southfield, but was that just the beginning? Would this turn into an all-out civil war?

As he walked along Interstate 94 he thought about the future. What would it mean if the United States broke up? The New Republic was aiming to make their own country out of the agrarian sector, so that would take Michigan, Minnesota, Wisconsin, Illinois, Iowa, Indiana, and Ohio. What would happen to rest of the states? The south had been threatening to leave for years. He thought about his history classes in high school. It was an American school so he had learned American history. The U.S. civil war was 200 years ago, but could it happen again? These thoughts rolled through his mind as he walked all day and into the night. Eventually he ended up in a campground. There were lights in the distance but he didn't want to risk going into a town. He went as far back into the campground as he could before making a fire; it got pretty cold at night. He stretched out on the ground, looking up at the stars. It was peaceful here, serene. He lifted his hand up in the air and traced the constellations he knew; Orion's Belt, the Big Dipper, and Little Dipper. Eventually he grew tired and fell asleep.

The first noise he heard when he awoke was gunfire. He bolted up, looking around. There were tanks rumbling down the highway. They had "Libertatum" spray painted in black, uneven lettering on the side. Men were standing up in them, firing their guns into the air. He grabbed his backpack and rose slowly to a crouched position and then shuffled behind a nearby tree. He leaned out slightly to assess the situation.

There were pick-up trucks following the tanks with men in the back, but they appeared to be prisoners from their down trodden faces. Ben tried to steady his breathing. His heart was racing. Adrenaline was pumping. One of the trucks rolled to a stop.

"Hey! I think there's someone over there, in the campground. That fire is recent."

Ben heard heavy footsteps coming toward him. He didn't have any options. He was alone with only a knife. He came out slowly from behind the tree with his arms raised above his head.

"Don't shoot. I'm not with the government."

He came face to face with the rebel. The guy couldn't have been older than nineteen. His eyes were bright, filled with youthful enthusiasm, and his facial hair was spotty.

"All right, all right. Let's just see who you are."

He kept an eye on Ben as he reached for Ben's bag. He pulled out the wallet and quickly found his driving license. It was from Beirut. "So you're Middle Eastern then?" he said, eyeing Ben skeptically.

"No, no. I'm American. I'm just visiting. I mean I was raised there but I was born here."

The rebel held his hand up to quiet Ben, and then yelled back at his partner in the truck.

"Hey, Matt, run this guy's name through the system. Benjamin Reginald Hughes. He says he's American."

"Sure thing."

Ben had left his passport at his cousins' house while he went on interviews, but they would know who he was soon enough.

"Yeah, he's American but his dad is, oh shit, his dad is the Ambassador to Lebanon. He's on the green list!"

"All right buddy, you're coming with me. You're a very important guy."

The rebel grabbed Ben's arm, leading him toward the truck. Ben did not struggle, but said, "He's not the Ambassador; he's Attaché to the Ambassador. It's not the same..."

"Whatever, you're government and high up. We could use a prisoner like you. You're on the green list, very important."

When they reached the truck, Ben was handcuffed behind his back and hoisted into the back with the rest of the prisoners. None of them would make eye contact with him.

"Hey, do you know where we're going?" Ben whispered to the prisoner next to him, a guy in his mid-fifties with glasses, wearing a suit. The man shook his head and looked away. For the next three hours they rumbled down the highway. They were heading south, leaving Michigan. Eventually they turned onto a dirt road and into an open field. There, the two tanks and four trucks parked in a circle.

One of the rebels in the first tank jumped down. He had a megaphone.

"Okay, everybody out. Let's set up camp."

Ben watched as more than two dozen rebels poured out of the tanks and trucks to set up camp. They pitched tents and built a fire in the center of the circle. The rebel who had caught him banged on the side of their truck, next to Ben.

"All right Ben Hughes, come out. We need you to make a phone call."

Ben stood up and weaved his way through the seated prisoners, then climbed out of the back of the truck. The rebel grabbed hold of his arm, leading him toward a tent on the opposite side of the circle. As they approached, the rebel with the megaphone from the first tank, who was waiting in the tent, smiled at them.

He addressed the rebel holding Ben, "Very good, Travis. I'll take it from here." Travis let go of Ben's arm, undid the handcuffs, and shoved him into the tent.

"Have a seat son," the rebel said. "We won't hurt you. You're too valuable to us, to our cause."

Ben sat down on the foldable chair set up next to a card table in the tent.

The rebel emptied a bag of devices, cell phones, tablets, and cameras, onto the card table. He turned a few of them over until he saw Ben's. It was marked with a green stamp.

"Okay, so we're going to turn on your phone and I need you to call your father and tell him that you've been captured. You're all right but he needs to urge the President to recognize the New Republic or you may not be all right anymore. Got that?"

Ben nodded, "Yes. You should know though, sir, that he's not the Ambassador. He doesn't have as much power as you think he does."

"We'll see about that. The leader put you and your family on the green list. Do you know what that means?"

Ben shook his head.

"It means you have direct influence in the White House. That means you do have power, and we intend to use it. Now, make that call. Make it short. We've got the government monitoring system so it won't be traced."

The rebel slid the phone across the table to Ben, who picked it up and turned it on. The screen lit up and he saw that he had eighteen new messages. It appeared that the rebels' "monitoring system" wasn't as sound as they thought. He didn't check the messages, but dialed his father's office number which was forwarded to his cell phone if there was no answer. He held the phone up to his ear; there were long pauses between rings, after four rings, his father answered. He was speaking Arabic, Ben instinctively answered in Arabic. The rebel held up his gun, "In English!" he yelled.

"Hi Dad, I've been captured by the rebels. I'm fine but you need to urge President Warren to recognize the New Republic. Good bye. I love you." He waited for a second before hanging up and he heard his father say, in Arabic, *El bakah honaykah* meaning "stay there."

He put the phone on the table. The rebel picked it up and turned it off.

"Very good, thank you. The leader will be very pleased. Now stand up." Ben stood and the rebel re-handcuffed him. "You'll be staying in the big tent back there, with the rest of the prisoners. Travis will let you know if we need any more of your help." He motioned for Ben to leave.

Ben shuffled out of the tent and walked toward the back of the circle. It was still day time but he was tired. Travis was waiting at the tent entrance.

"Thanks a lot, green list," he said, patting Ben on the back. "Sit any-

74

where, we'll be here for a while."

Ben sat next to the same man he had been next to in the truck. Of all the prisoners, he looked the least shell shocked.

"Hey, do you know where they're taking us?"

The man acted like he didn't hear him.

"Can you hear me?"

The man turned and looked him directly in the eye, "Yes, I can hear you."

"So do you know what's going on?"

The man nodded, "We are all green list in this group. We'll most likely be tortured until we tell them what they want to hear."

"And what's that?"

"Crimes we've committed, connections to other government officials."

"But I haven't done anything."

The man shook his head, "It doesn't matter. In situations like this, everything is binary. Either you're a good guy or you're a bad guy."

"And why did they take you? Did you work for the government?"

"Yes, I was the Attorney General. I'm John Caring."

Ben nodded; he had heard the name but he hadn't spent much time in Michigan, so it didn't mean much to him.

The guards moved between them. John Caring turned away from

Ben and put his head down between his knees. Ben wondered if he had been tortured already. Several hours passed before the sun went down. No one brought them food or water. Ben drifted in and out of sleep.

In the middle of the night he heard something outside the tent, rustling, footsteps. Was someone whispering? It was faint; it could have been the wind. He looked to the entrance of the tent where Travis was sitting on a foldable chair, guarding them. Something was off, his body was slumped oddly. Then he saw it, a dart or syringe sticking out of his neck. The back of the tent opened and two men came in, dressed in all back, crouched low to the ground. They held their fingers to their lips to indicate silence. All the prisoners glanced up. The men moved through the prisoners, looking at them one by one until they got to Ben. Then one man whispered to him in Arabic, as the other lifted him to his feet. They were mercenaries. His father had sent them. They nodded to him and then he followed them slowly out of the back of the tent, past the trucks and out into the night.

They ran through a field until they got to the interstate. A car was waiting, and a third man was in the driver's seat. The mercenaries got in the back seat and motioned for Ben to get in the front. The driver leaned over and opened the door for him. He was older, maybe in his mid-sixties. He was tan, balding and slightly overweight, and he had a fatherly, reassuring smile.

"Hello, Mr. Hughes. How are you? Are you well?"

Ben got in the car and closed the door, "Yes, I'm fine. Do you have any water?"

"Yes, at your feet."

Ben reached down and took a water bottle from the cooler at his feet. He drank and instantly felt better. The driver put the car in gear and turned onto the interstate. "Where are we going?"

"There is a helicopter which will be arriving momentarily. Just five miles away. We have your cousins too, don't worry."

"And my father arranged all of this?"

"Yes, he is a good man, your father. We go back a long time. And you, my son, are very fortunate. They are doing terrible things to those prisoners. You are very lucky to be alive."

"I was only captured yesterday."

"Praise Allah."

Ben nodded. The driver had a faint Lebanese accent, like some of the diplomats he had grown up around, but he had never seen this man before. He had no idea his father had these kind of connections in the United States. A few minutes later they pulled into a parking lot, and then the helicopter arrived. The driver remained in the car. He lived in Indiana, apparently. The two mercenaries left with Ben, and his cousins were waiting in the helicopter. They flew to New York, where they took a private plane to Lebanon. Ben stayed there, with his family, until the war was over.

January 1, 2061

PROCLAMATION IV

Dear citizens,

I, Winston Huang, appreciate the expediency with which you have registered in the New Republic. As you will shortly be assigned to your housing units, I will at this time explain the five fundamental regulations we must all live by to create a more fruitful, efficient, and effective society. Failure to comply with these regulations will result in penalties, and possible incarceration.

Five Regulations of the New Republic

· Housing - Assigned housing units are based on need. They have been assigned fairly and without malice. There is no option to transfer.

· Curfew - Curfew for all citizens is 11 pm Central Standard Time. Only personnel performing work related duties for the government of the New Republic may be outside of their housing units after 11 pm. There are no exceptions.

· Communications - All telephone calls must be limited to five minutes and may be reviewed by the appropriate authorities if they are found to contain inflammatory language or language that undermines the New Republic. All text exchanges must be kept to fewer than 500 words and will be reviewed as well.

· Employment - Work assignments will be made on a rolling basis. You may apply to open positions based on your education and work experience. Those who have already received their work assignments will begin work on the date specified in their employment letters. There are no work transfers at this time. You are allowed to apply for a transfer, within the same field, no sooner than one calendar year after beginning your work assignment.

· Civil Society - You are responsible for your own safety and the safety of your fellow citizens. If you suspect that someone is participating in acts or exhibiting behavior that undermines the New Republic, it is your civic duty to report them to the appropriate authorities. Compensation may be given to those citizens who comply with this regulation.

In addition, all prisoners who were taken during the uprising and War of Autonomy are in the Federal Penitentiary in Detroit. They are awaiting trial. Their trials will be held at the Federal Courthouse of Honor and Liberty in Detroit. Any citizen wishing to inquire as to the status of a prisoner can file the appropriate form at the registration office in their district.

I look forward to our growth and achievements as one equal, cohesive society.

Sincerely,

Winston Huang

Honorable General and President of the New Republic

Life in the New Republic: Part I

January 5, 2061

Emily Caring stood in line, waiting to leave the refugee camp for good. She was holding her registration card, housing assignment, and work assignment. Emily was assigned to an apartment with her mother and Wallace, and a job teaching first grade at an elementary school just a short bus ride away from their apartment. Everything on paper looked normal, but she feared it wasn't. She hadn't been in contact with her family at all. They were on her contacts list but she hadn't heard from them. Would they really be at the apartment when she got there? Was this all a trap? Where were Daniel and her father? She had been lucky so far, she had to remember that. She had survived the war unscathed and had received a housing unit with her family and a work assignment. She just had so many questions.

The guard at the gate held out his hand, "Registration card and any other paperwork."

He wore traditional military fatigues but there was a black band around his right arm.

Emily handed him her card and paperwork.

"Thank you Miss Caring."

She nodded at him, without making eye contact.

"Since your housing and work assignments are in Detroit, you will be taking the courtesy bus there. The buses are organized by number. Go to bus number 11 when you exit. Seats are not assigned."

She started to walk away, when the guard gently clasped her arm.

"Emily, it's me," he whispered.

Her eyes darted up. She scanned his face. He did look vaguely familiar but she couldn't place him. She had seen so many of the same faces in the camp for the last four years that memories of people in her past were fading away. Sometimes she couldn't even picture her parents.

"It's me, Kyle. We were in gym class together in high school, Mr. Herzog's class, freshman year."

He had changed a lot between fifteen and twenty-five years old, but she did recognize him. She smiled, but almost immediately her eyes clouded with sadness. He had joined the revolution. He was a soldier in the New Republic. "Don't worry, when I saw your name I checked. You have nice housing. I'm stationed in your district, so if you ever need anything, please let me know." His smile was reassuring, but Emily didn't know what to say. If he was a revolutionary she couldn't trust him.

"Sure, I will. Thank you," she replied quietly.

He turned to address the next refugee as she moved past him and left the camp.

Outside it was freezing, a typical January day in Michigan. Now it wasn't "Michigan" though. It was the New Republic, which included most of the former Midwest. Emily wrapped her arms around herself tightly, trying to insulate from the cold. The wind whipped her hair in front of her face as she gazed up at the dozen or so buses lined up to take refugees to Detroit. Each bus had a number hanging from inside the front window. They weren't lined up chronologically; bus number 11 was third from the left. She made her way to the bus slowly, battling the wind. When she got there the driver opened the door and glanced down at her. She held up her registration card and the driver nodded his approval. Then Emily climbed the steps and faced the aisle. The bus was mostly empty. The few passengers were in window seats, gazing out. She found a single seat near the back and sat down, holding her backpack on her lap. After twenty or so minutes, the bus lurched forward and slowly left the parking lot, eventually reaching the interstate and heading for Detroit.

As they approached Detroit, Emily expected to see destruction, bombed out buildings, and tanks—a war zone. Instead, everything looked pretty much the same. Most of the buildings were intact. The flag of the New Republic was hung on the flag poles in front of schools and some private homes.

Soon she realized they were heading toward the Detroit River. Several new apartment buildings had been built along the riverfront after the 2025 riots. The riverfront was still beautiful and reminded her of home. The bus slowed down as they approached the corner of St. Anne and Lafayette Boulevards.

The driver's voice came on over the loudspeaker, "Okay, this is your stop. Bring your housing assignment numbers up here to Delora, and she'll tell you which building and apartment you're in, and give you your keys." Emily stood up and walked in line behind the other passengers waiting to exit the bus.

At the front Delora, a young, bubbly blonde woman, was standing holding a tablet. There was a box of keys next to her on the dashboard.

"Name?" Delora's tone was upbeat, the most cheerful tone Emily had heard from anyone in over four years. It bothered her.

"Emily Caring."

"Housing number?"

Emily read the number from her housing assignment, "1029794."

Delora smiled at her, tapped on the tablet and then reached around to the box of keys, rummaging for a bit, and then producing a padded envelope. "Okay, Emily! Here are your keys. Your new address is 2533 Lafayette Boulevard, just a couple blocks away! You're in apartment number 6. I can see here that Catherine and Wallace Caring have already checked in, so you're all set."

Emily's heart skipped a beat. Her mother and Wallace were already there. She grabbed the envelope from Delora, ran down the steps of the bus and sprinted up Lafayette Boulevard.

She was looking at each building she passed, "2651, 2603" the buildings were a blur as she ran but she knew she was almost there.

"2533 Lafayette."

The building had large metallic letters decorating its front façade, declaring its address.

Emily raced into the lobby of the building, slowing down once she got inside. Her eyes darted back and forth, looking for a stairwell or elevator. The stairs were to her left. She leapt up them two at a time. It was only a two story building, so at the top she saw Apartment Number 1. She walked down the hallway until she reached Number 6. She could hear noise from inside the apartment. Her heart was pounding. She rapped using the door knocker.

She heard footsteps and then the door swung open. Her mother stood there and as soon as she saw Emily, she burst into tears and pulled her into an embrace. Her mother's hair was gray; before the war, Emily had never seen a gray hair on her head. Emily broke down into sobs too, but her head was up so she could see Wallace, who had come next to Emily and was hugging them both. He was much taller than the last time she had seen him and bigger too. He was a man.

They all cried and hugged for a few minutes and then Emily released them. She had to know what had happened to her father and Daniel. Her mother led her into the modest apartment. It had two bedrooms, a living room, kitchen, and a bathroom. She and her mother would be sharing a room, and Wallace would be in the other room.

The living room furniture was plain and clearly used. There was a faded olive green couch and two matching chairs. Emily and Wallace sat in the chairs across from their mother, who was on the couch.

"So what happened? Where are dad and Daniel?"

Catherine Caring sat with her hands clasped over her crossed legs. She took a deep breath, and began. "The soldiers came about an hour after you left for Aunt Caroline's. They knew when your father would be home; he'd only been home for about five minutes when they showed up. They had a list with all of our names on it, including yours. Your father went quietly, but Daniel... he fought back. Wallace tried to stop him, but the rebels, they attacked him."

She started crying, but as soon as Emily attempted to comfort her she waved her hand in front of her face to signal that she was fine.

"No, no I'm okay. Let me finish. They shot Daniel and they wouldn't let us take his body. I don't know where he is but we assume he's dead. Your father was taken to prison, and Wallace and I were taken to 'private housing' in Wisconsin."

"Don't let anyone hear you say that," Wallace interrupted. "The place could be bugged."

Catherine nodded, "In what used to be Wisconsin. We're in the New Republic now."

"So we don't know what happened to Daniel, and dad is in the federal prison, here in Detroit?"

"Yes, that's correct," Catherine replied and Wallace nodded.

Emily took a minute to process what she had just heard. She nodded slowly. "What is private housing?"

Catherine looked around, like she was waiting for someone to walk in and say, "We can hear you!"

"Mom?"

Her mother leaned in and whispered, "It's an internment camp. I sewed black arm bands and flags. Wallace made weapons."

Emily nodded.

"So, how are you?" Wallace asked Emily hesitatingly.

"I'm well, very happy to be here with you both," Emily smiled. Her time at the refugee camp hadn't been bad at all. She was grateful now that she had been there, instead of an internment camp.

"I was an elementary school teacher at the refugee camp. I had my own tent and I made a few friends. No one that was given a housing placement near here, but I'm hoping after we settle in a little bit that maybe we can visit each other. We'll see."

Her voice trailed off. All of sudden, she thought about Ben — the guy she had met on the way to the camp. She had never called his cousins' house. She was too afraid during the war.

"So, how about some dinner?" Catherine's voice was cheerful.

"That sounds great, thanks mom," said Emily. "So we have food, dishes and everything?"

"Yes, the government was very helpful. All the apartments are fully furnished, and we were able to buy food with the money we earned in private housing."

"Great. Well what can I do to help?"

"I put a pot roast on earlier, so dinner's almost ready, but you can set the table. That would be very helpful." Her mother gave her another hug and kissed her forehead before going into the kitchen.

Emily looked to Wallace. "So is everything really okay? Is mom okay?" Emily whispered.

"As much as she can be, I guess. The first year was really hard on her. She kept asking about you, dad and Daniel, no one would give her any answers. They put her in solitary confinement for a while. Eventually she calmed down and just kept working, we'd eat dinner together every night. She read a lot. Once she found out you were okay, that made a huge difference."

"When was that? When did she find out about me?"

"Oh, I don't know maybe two years ago? One of the guards told her you were in a camp. They wouldn't say which one, but he told her you had been there for over a year and that you were fine. That changed her for sure. She seemed more hopeful after that. Then about a month ago she got word that dad was in prison. That helped her too. She's better now than she's been since the war started."

"I put you guys on my contacts list at the registration office, didn't they tell you?"

"No," Wallace shook his head.

Emily nodded, "So what about you? How are you doing?"

Wallace paused, taking in the question. "I'm good. I actually, sorry, I know I shouldn't be thinking about this, but... there's this girl I met in private housing, her name is Hillary. She was placed here in Detroit with her family too; which is weird because they're from St. Louis, but whatever. She's close and I want to see her tonight, but I don't know how because I know mom wants me here, and you just got here..."

Emily laughed.

"What?"

"It's just funny, that life can be so normal again so fast."

"This is not normal."

"Yes, it is. We're all living together and you have a new girlfriend, and that's the problem we're discussing. I'm not wondering if you're alive or dead, or if I'll ever see you again."

"Sure, I mean yes, but do you think mom will let me leave after dinner and go see her? We all have to be in by 11 pm, so maybe just for an hour?"

Emily smiled reassuringly, "Yeah, I'm sure it will be fine. I'm fine with it. Don't worry."

"Oh, okay good. I thought you might be mad because you just got here."

Emily shook her head, "Listen, it is fine. It's only a couple hours and then we'll be living here for who knows how long."

Wallace nodded, smiling, "You're the best, thank you. I'll wait until after dinner and then tell mom." He gave Emily a hug, and then they both went into the kitchen to get the dishes and set the table.

———

The next morning, Emily woke up to the smell of coffee. Her mother was already up and out of bed. There were two twin beds in their room. They were old, but they were clean and the sheets were new. The night before she had watched her mother reading before bed; she looked so much older than four years ago, but her presence was the same. She was calm, reserved, reading a Jane Austen novel with her reading glasses pushed down her nose. Her mother's energy made the room peaceful and Emily had quickly and easily fallen asleep. She had slept deeply and felt well rested.

Emily climbed out of bed and when she got to the kitchen she saw Wallace seated at the table, reading the newspaper. It struck her how much he looked like Daniel. Wallace was the same size Daniel had been the last time she had seen him.

"Good morning," she said cheerfully.

Wallace looked up and nodded.

"What are you reading?"

"France and Germany have recognized the restructuring. The British will still only speak with President Warren, but since he's only in charge of the United North, it's just a matter of time."

Wallace spread the paper out on the table. There was a map of the former United States, each new region was divided by color and the countries which had recognized them were listed on the side. Emily had seen this map before. It had gone up in the camp a few months ago, when they heard the end of the war was near. There were five new countries created from the former United States, known collectively as "The Five."

The Five

1. **New Republic:** Michigan, Minnesota, Wisconsin, Illinois, Iowa, Indiana, and Ohio.

2. **Texas**

3. **Confederacy:** Missouri, Arkansas, Kentucky, Tennessee, Louisiana, Mississippi, Alabama, Georgia, Florida, North Carolina, South Carolina, and West Virginia.

4. **United North:** Virginia, Washington D.C., Pennsylvania, Maryland, Delaware, New Jersey, New York, Connecticut, Vermont, Massachusetts, New Hampshire, and Maine.

5. **Northwest America:** North Dakota, South Dakota, Nebraska, Kansas, Oklahoma, New Mexico, Colorado, Wyoming, Montana, Idaho, Utah, Arizona, Nevada, California, Oregon, and Washington.

Hawaii had become an independent kingdom again, and Canada had taken over Alaska during the war. Emily had to teach this new map to the children in her class. It must have been how teachers felt after World War I, when the world map no longer included "empires." The Ottoman Empire had been broken up into numerous countries in Europe and North Africa. New maps had been made then, and they would be made now. School started on Monday, January 17, but orientation for new teachers began this Monday, January 10. Just four days away.

"Do you actually think this will last?" Emily said, gesturing to the map.

Wallace pondered the question for a minute, "Yes, I do. They spent four years fighting for it and they won. Maybe not everyone's happy with the outcome but I think people are sick of fighting, they're sick of war, and they just want to move on with their lives. What about you though? How come you're working and not finishing school?"

"They sent me a diploma actually. I was only two credits short and they said my work in the camp counted as credit. A few of the refugees around my age were sent diplomas. I guess they figured we were so close to graduating, and we had lost four years anyway. I do want to go back though and go to grad school, maybe law school like dad."

Wallace nodded.

"What about you? You're starting school next week, right?"

"Not exactly, it's the military academy. Since I missed my mandatory year, I'm doing it now but taking some classes too. I'm not sure what I get at the end. They said I get a certificate, but what does that even mean in the grand scheme of things? Does that mean I'll get college credit? And what colleges will take it?"

"I don't know... where's mom?"

"She's out taking a walk. She's been doing that too, taking long walks in the morning."

Just as Wallace said that, they heard keys rattling, and then the front door opened and closed. Catherine entered the kitchen. "Good morning my little loves!" She hugged them both, Emily noticeably longer.

"How was your walk, mom?" asked Wallace.

"It was nice, brisk. It's cold out there."

Emily noticed her mother's hands were shaking slightly, probably from the cold.

"Have you had any coffee?" her mother asked her.

"No, not yet."

"Let's have some together then," she smiled and squeezed Emily's arm.

It was all so normal, natural and safe, but at the same time it wasn't. Emily's world had changed rapidly in the last twenty-four hours, and she knew this was just the beginning.

January 6, 2061

"Please step up to the red line, face the camera, state your name, age and date of birth," the guard waved Ben up to the line.

"Benjamin Hughes, age 29, November 27, 2031."

Several people came after him, and eventually Anabelle, Christopher, and their parents were called.

"Step up closer miss, we can't hear you."

"Annabelle Stevenson, age 25, April 9, 2035."

"Christopher Stevenson, age 21, December 2, 2039."

"Isabelle Stevenson, age 65, July 28, 1995."

"Michael Stevenson, age 65, June 12, 1995."

They stood there, on a red line on the floor, facing the camera, each holding their registration card and saying their names, ages, and dates of birth, before having their picture taken for the database.

The Stevenson family had returned to the country after being promised new housing and a job assignment for Michael. Also, Canada wouldn't house them anymore. Refugees who were not asylum seekers had to return to their home countries. It was the law.

Ben had returned because after his experience with the rebels he wanted to fight back. This "New Republic" was unjust and he knew it could not last. He wanted to fight from the inside, get elected to public office and change things legally and logistically. Over the past four years he had studied law and was prepared to take the bar exam. He couldn't let this new government continue very long as it was, and he knew exactly where to start—the capital, Detroit.

———

The Stevensons stepped off the bus onto Lafayette Boulevard, on the riverfront.

"It's been a long time since we've been here," Annabelle whispered to Christopher, remembering their trip across the Detroit River to Canada four years earlier.

"It certainly looks different," Christopher replied.

"What are you kids whispering about? Grab those boxes and let's go inside."

Isabelle Stevenson hadn't been the same since the war. She was abrupt now, curt, and always suspicious. Perhaps it was the guilt she felt for leaving her children alone when the rebels came, or the fact that she and her husband had the same qualifications, but he had been offered a job and she hadn't. They both had doctorates in environmental science. She knew how important the work they were doing before the war was to the government, but only Michael had a job.

She and Michael had found out where Annabelle and Christopher were as soon as the Canadian refugee registry had been posted online. For two months they had been staying near the U.S. Embassy in Rome, checking every day for news of the war and its survivors. As soon as they heard, they had flown to Canada and stayed in refugee housing, as a family, until the war was over.

They had been assigned to a building called The Waterfront at 2600 Lafayette Boulevard. Their apartment was on the first floor, Apartment A. They were told it was a three bedroom apartment with "adequate room for four people." The flag of the New Republic hung outside. When they entered the lobby, there was a large sign welcoming them, and all returning citizens, to their new home and their new country.

Their apartment faced an interior courtyard. Isabelle took the keys out of the padded envelope, turned the lock and opened the door. It was much smaller than they had imagined. It was clear that it had been a two bedroom, with one bedroom divided into two with a thin, plastic wall. The walls were a dingy off-white color. The kitchen appliances had been hastily installed. There were flecks of paint on them. The place was cheap but clean.

They had all been housed together and Michael would begin his new job the next day. He had been assigned a position in the Department of the Interior. Since they had been on vacation when the war broke out, the Stevensons hadn't been flagged as fleeing the country, and the government had been remarkably lenient about Christopher shooting the soldiers when they tried to take Annabelle. Christopher had been pardoned because he had acted "in self-defense and under duress." Annabelle hadn't been charged at all, and it seemed they were unaware of their escape route to Canada, which made sense since they hadn't been caught.

"Okay, well, let's unpack." Isabelle sighed, and put her hands on her hips.

Christopher put down the two boxes he was carrying, took out his pocket knife and opened them. They contained some winter clothes and framed pictures of their family. They had been given these boxes at the registration office when they returned from Canada. They were filled with items that had been retrieved from their former house in Woodland Hills. Clearly, the government had expected them to return. Only a few families had boxes waiting for them.

"Mom, where should I put this stuff?" Christopher held up his mother's diploma and a picture of his grandparents, both were in large, gold frames.

"Leave those in the box, I'll hang them up later. Just put the winter coats in the closet, and take anything that's yours to your room. Annabelle, you do the same."

Annabelle nodded, and she and Christopher headed back to the bedroom which had been divided into two. "So which side do you want? The one with the window or the one with the closet?" Annabelle asked.

"Doesn't matter. Window, I guess. If you don't mind not having any natural light?"

"Oh, I'll get some light." Annabelle gestured to the ceiling, there was a clear plastic strip at the top of the make shift wall. "It will filter in from your room."

Christopher chuckled, "Okay, cool. I'll take this room then, and you take the one on the left. Wait, where will I hang up my clothes?"

"We can share my closet, don't worry."

"Thanks."

Clean sheets were folded on top of their beds, and they both instinctively began unfolding them and making their respective beds. When they were done, Christopher came over to Annabelle's room and sat down.

"So what do you think they'll have dad doing?"

"I have no idea. His focus was on water conservation, but now, who knows?"

"Do you think he'll actually meet General Huang?"

They both sat in silence for a minute, remembering when they had seen the general murder Governor Adams by Ambassador Bridge. If he had been capable of that, who knew what else he was capable of?

"Kids, are you all done in there?"

"Almost, do you need something?"

"No, just checking. Your father and I are going to head to the grocery store and pick up a few things, would you like to come?"

Annabelle looked at Christopher who rolled his eyes. Their mother had been like that ever since they had been reunited in Canada. She didn't want them out of her sight, ever. They were adults and she still called them kids.

"No, that's okay. We'll just stay here," Christopher replied.

"Okay, well if you're sure. We won't be gone long, maybe an hour at the most."

"Great, thanks, mom. Bye guys."

––––––

Ben had arrived in the New Republic alone. His family, including his cousins, had chosen to stay in Lebanon. His father had gotten a job offer from the United North to become the Ambassador to Lebanon. It was a big promotion and since the United North was the only country from the former United States to have an embassy in the Middle East, it was important. The other new countries had yet to define their foreign policies. Aside from the United North, which was retaining most of the embassies formerly held by the United States, only Texas had established a foreign embassy in Mexico City.

At the registration office, Ben declared his citizenship in the New Republic and asked for a housing assignment in Detroit. Surprisingly, they had an opening. If he were willing to help manage the building, he could have an apartment at 2533 Lafayette Boulevard. Apparently, the assigned manager was having difficulty keeping up with the paperwork. With Ben's legal background and engineering degrees, the housing assignment officer thought he would be a perfect fit. It was that, or Ben would be sent to one of the former refugee camps to await a different housing assignment, which could take months. He agreed to manage the building.

"Fantastic!" said the housing assignment officer, a girl with bright red hair whose effusive personality bothered Ben. There was no way she was this excited to give him a housing assignment. It seemed contrived. He nodded and took the piece of paper from her.

"So you can just head outside and take bus number five to your new neighborhood. It's right on the riverfront, beautiful area."

"Okay, thanks."

"Thank *you!*"

It was odd. The soldiers in the New Republic were stern, but the office and administration workers were all bubbly and effusive. Something was off.

When he got outside the wind hit him hard; he had forgotten how cold it was here in the winter. He didn't have a proper coat so he bent over, bracing himself against the wind. When he got to bus number five, he knocked and the doors opened. He looked up and couldn't believe who he saw in the driver's seat. It was Travis, the rebel who had captured him four years ago. Ben climbed up the steps, waiting for some sign of recognition from him, but Travis just stared blankly ahead.

"Take any open seat; we'll leave in ten minutes."

Ben nodded and sat near the front so he could be one of the first people off the bus. He gazed out from the window at the dozens of people coming out of the registration office and boarding different buses. After the bus was full, Travis closed the doors and the bus pulled out of the parking lot and onto the highway.

Growing up, Ben had always wondered what it would be like to live in the United States, but he was living in the New Republic now. Everything was different. He could have applied for citizenship in the United North, and easily gotten it with his father's connections, but he wanted to come here and fix the New Republic. And he had been thinking about Emily for the past four years.

The bus slowed to a stop at the corner of St. Anne and Lafayette Boulevards. As instructed, Ben went to the front with his housing assignment to get his keys.

"Since you're the assistant manager of the building, you have a set of maintenance keys as well. You have access to the boiler room, electric switchboard, and the administrative office."

"Yes, thank you," Ben replied.

He took the padded envelope and walked down the steps to the sidewalk. As he walked up Lafayette Boulevard, he could see Ambassador Bridge just a block away. The flag of the New Republic flew from its top spire on the American side. It was bizarre to see a flag other than that of the United States. He turned his attention to the numbers on the buildings; he was almost there. Eventually, he saw a grey building with "2533 Lafayette" in large gold lettering on the front. He crossed the street and walked up to the building. The front doors were unlocked. That would have to change. He went inside and into the lobby, he walked down the hall past the elevator and laundry room, until he got to a door with the letter A on it. *This must be it* he thought.

He pulled his keys out of the padded envelope, trying each one until the door opened with the fourth key. The room was small, barely a studio apartment. There were hardwood floors, a bed in the corner, a small closet, and a bathroom. There wasn't a kitchen, just a mini refrigerator with a small microwave on top of it. Ben put his backpack down and sat on the edge of the bed. His parents would be sending two boxes of books and his suits from Lebanon as soon as they had his address. Hopefully his belongings would arrive next week.

———

January 8, 2061

Emily was taking her first trip to the grocery store. She hadn't been in a store in over four years. Her mother had encouraged her to come along.

"Come on, it will be fun. We can go together, like we used to when you were little."

Emily had agreed and so here they were, walking down the stairs to leave their apartment building. When they got to the lobby Emily couldn't believe her eyes. Walking in the front door to the building was Ben, the guy she had spent the night with in the warehouse on her journey to the refugee camp.

Ben stopped and stared at her too. "Emily Johnson!" he exclaimed.

Her mother looked at her, quizzically.

"It's Emily Caring, actually. Sorry, I lied before," Emily blurted out.

Ben took it in stride, "Oh, okay, well hello Emily Caring. And I would assume this is your mother?"

"Yes, sorry. This is my mother, Catherine Caring." Emily turned to her mother, "Mom, this is Benjamin Hughes. We met when I was going to the refugee camp... I spent the night in a warehouse and Ben was there too."

Catherine raised her eyebrows slightly, then turned to Ben. "It's very nice to meet you, Ben. Are you living in this building?"

"Yes, I'm the assistant manager."

"So you're with the revolution? I mean, the government?"

"No, ma'am. Well I hope to be, this was the quickest housing assignment they could give me. I came from Lebanon, my father's the American Ambassador there for the United... North."

"And you chose to come back here?"

"Yes, ma'am. I'm taking the bar exam next week, and I'm hoping to run for public office."

"Oh, how industrious of you. My husband was in public office. He was the Attorney General here, in Michigan." At this Emily and her mother both paused. They hadn't discussed John Caring with anyone.

Ben noted their discomfort, and nodded. "That's great. I'd love to meet him sometime."

"Yes, that would be nice," Emily replied, while her mother smiled uncomfortably.

"Okay, well we're off to the grocery store. It was very nice to meet you, Benjamin, and I'm sure we'll see you soon."

"Very nice to meet you too, Mrs. Caring." Ben smiled, and Emily felt herself blush. "Emily, nice to see you again."

After they got outside, Catherine turned to Emily while they walked. "So how do you know him?"

"Well, when I was traveling from the house to the refugee camp, I stopped for a night at a warehouse a few miles away. It looked abandoned, I mean it was abandoned, but then Ben arrived. He was traveling too, back to his cousins' house in Indiana. I had no idea he was from Lebanon. I think he mentioned he wasn't from here or that he had lived abroad. I don't remember exactly. He was really nice though," at this Emily paused, remembering how Ben had gazed at her when she walked down the stairs that morning four years ago. "He made me oatmeal and coffee, and he told me jokes."

"Can he be trusted?"

"I think so."

"Well good. If he's serious about running for public office, and he's living in our building, he could be an asset."

"An asset?"

"Yes, of course. For getting your father freed. If he goes to trial, he could end up in prison, permanently, or worse."

Emily gasped, "You don't think they'd have him executed? He hasn't done anything wrong."

"I have no idea, but we need to prepare for the worst. I never thought a lot of things would happen. I never thought there would be a civil war. I never thought the United States would break up. I never thought I'd be living in government housing while my son was missing and my husband was in prison. If your grandparents were alive..." at this Catherine trailed off, shaking her head. Then her tone changed, like she had been snapped back to the present. "Well look at that, we're almost at the grocery store." She grasped Emily's hand for a moment.

Emily had noticed that her mother did that from time to time. She would get lost in a memory or a thought and then, as if she had flipped an internal switch, she would snap back out of it and her tone would transform into one of purpose. And if Emily were close, she would grasp her hand.

They crossed the street and went into the grocery store.

———

January 10, 2061

"Do you have everything you need?"

"Yes, mom."

"You have the lunch I packed for you and the bus pass Wallace got from the registration office?"

"Yes, mom."

"Okay, good."

It was Emily's first day of teacher orientation at her new school, and the first time since they had been reunited that she would be away from Wallace and her mother. It was her first day on her own in the New Republic.

The bus stop was where they had been dropped off five days earlier at the corner of St. Anne and Lafayette Boulevards. Emily zipped up her coat, swung her backpack over her shoulder, gave her mother a hug, and headed out the door. Once she got to the stop there was a line already forming. The bus was set to arrive in eight minutes. A schedule had been automatically downloaded to her phone by the government. As she waited, she re-read that day's orientation schedule. Mostly it was introductions to the school and curriculum, with a long treatise she had read over the weekend. She wouldn't see her classroom until Wednesday.

When it was time to board the bus, she looked up from her phone and it hit her that she would officially be starting her job today. It was daunting. There were several people in front of her in line so by the time she boarded the bus it was almost full. She walked down the aisle slowly, looking for an open seat. Then she saw a famil-iar face. It was Annabelle Stevenson, her friend from elementary school. Annabelle was looking out the window, and the seat next to her was empty.

"Excuse me, Annabelle?" Emily's voice was hesitant.

Annabelle looked up and smiled widely when she saw it was Emily. "Emily, oh my God, hi! Please, sit next to me."

"Great, thank you," Emily smiled back.

"I can't believe you're here. How are you?"

Emily told Annabelle her war story, and Annabelle told Emily hers.

Annabelle left out the part about seeing Emily's father and watching General Huang murder the Governor. She hadn't spoken about that with anyone since that night.

"Wow. I can't believe you were in Canada."

"I can't believe you were in a refugee camp all alone, without your family. I don't know what I would have done."

Emily paused, "Well do you have a job then? Is that why you're heading downtown?"

"Yes, sort of. My dad got me an internship at the Ministry of the Interior. Since the whole college credit thing has to be worked out, he figured this would be a good opportunity in the interim."

Emily nodded.

"And so you're going to be a teacher or keep being a teacher that is. Don't you need to finish your degree?"

"Well I only had two credits left until I was done, so they said my work experience in the camp counted as credit and sent me my diploma. I think they just really need qualified teachers in the government schools."

"Oh that's good."

They were both silent for a moment. Finally, Emily spoke. "I'm really glad we ran into each other. We should hang out now that we're both back, and since we live in the same neighborhood. It would be great to see your family too."

"Absolutely, maybe you, your mom, and Wallace can come over for dinner this week? I'll have to check with my parents but I'm sure they would love it."

"That sounds great!"

The bus had come to a stop and people were starting to disembark. Emily and Annabelle quickly exchanged phone numbers. When they got off the bus they hugged.

"Good luck on your first day!"

"You too!"

Then each went to their new work assignments.

_____

January 14, 2061

"We'll be there at 7 o'clock. Should we bring anything?"

"Oh no, that's not necessary."

"I know my mother will insist that we bring something."

"Oh okay, well then a bottle of wine, red wine since we're having pasta."

"Great! Thank you. So it's just going to be our families, right?"

"Actually my dad invited a friend from work, this guy Andy. And he's bringing a friend too. Some guy he met during his mandatory year who's living in Detroit now."

"Oh, are they dating?"

"No, well I don't think so. I think my dad is trying to set me up with

Andy, actually. He's only a few years older than us."

Emily nodded to herself. She and Annabelle spoke on the phone every night and rode the bus together every morning. Their friendship had grown quickly. Even after several years apart, they were as close as they had been as children.

"Okay, red wine it is. I'll see you tomorrow night."

"Okay, bye."

———

January 15, 2061

"Welcome, come in, come in, I'm so glad the girls arranged this. Please, let me take your coats."

Isabelle Stevenson ushered in Catherine, Wallace, and then Emily.

"Thank you for having us. It's so nice to see you again, all of you." Catherine gazed around the room. Michael, Christopher and Annabelle were standing in the living room, smiling.

Isabelle disappeared into Christopher's bedroom with the coats. Catherine gave two bottles of wine to Michael.

"Thank you so much, Catherine, that's very considerate of you."

"Of course. So I hear you have a new job?"

"Yes, at the Department of the Interior." Michael shifted his weight uncomfortably.

"Working for the government."

"Yes, yes I am. General Huang is actually quite the conservationist."

Before Catherine could say anything, there was a knock at the door. Michael moved to open it.

"That must be the guys, excuse me." Michael opened the door and in walked Andy, tall, brunette, average-looking, and Ben.

Emily watched them come in and her eyes widened. Isabelle had returned and rushed over to take their coats.

Michael turned to the room to introduce them, "Everyone, this is Andy Seward, he's my assistant at the department, and who's your friend Andy?"

"I'm Ben, Benjamin Hughes."

"We've met actually," said Catherine. "Ben works in our apartment building, and he and Emily met during the war."

"Really? What a strange coincidence!" Michael exclaimed.

"Yes, well, Emily and I met each other one night on the road during the uprising. I'm the manager of the 2533 Lafayette building now. We ran into each other a few days ago, and I had the pleasure of meeting Catherine."

"You're the manager? I thought you were the assistant manager," Emily commented.

Ben chuckled, "The manager got fired. Apparently he liked to drink a little too much. I only found out yesterday that I'd been promoted."

"Well congratulations," said Catherine.

Annabelle gave Emily a look. They had discussed Ben at length and how Emily had a crush on him. "Should we open the wine?" Annabelle asked, rhetorically, as she had already taken out the glasses.

"Yes, let's!" exclaimed Isabelle. It was easy to tell how excited she was to be hosting a dinner party.

Annabelle poured nine glasses of wine, and Emily helped her pass them out. Wallace and Christopher were chatting in the corner, while Michael, Catherine and Isabelle were reminiscing.

Andy turned to Annabelle, "So, your father says you're an economics major?"

"I was an economics major. I'm not sure when I'll be returning to school."

"Well you're doing a great job at the department, at least that's what I hear."

Annabelle smiled, "From my father, I assume?"

Andy chuckled, nodding, "Yes and from other people. And I read your summary of your father's report on water conservation. It was excellent, very clear. I liked it."

Annabelle blushed. "Thank you."

"So what about you Emily? Are you working too?"

"Yes, I'm a first grade teacher."

"Oh really, how's that going?"

Emily shrugged, "So far, so good. Last week was just orientation.

The kids arrive on Monday. Then we'll see. I taught at a refugee camp during the war so I'm not nervous about the teaching itself, it's the curriculum. It's so different from what we learned in school."

"How so?"

Emily paused and looked to Ben. She realized she wasn't sure what Andy believed in, if he were a revolutionary or one of them—a loyalist to the former United States. Ben smiled at her and nodded, understanding her dilemma by her silence.

"It's okay," said Ben. "Andy isn't a revolutionary."

"Oh God no!" Andy said. "I didn't mean to pry. Believe me, I can only imagine what they're having you teach. Revised history and all that."

"Yes! It's all so strange. They make the war seem like a good thing, a great thing," Emily said.

"It's okay, I get it. We all get it." Ben put his hand on Emily's shoulder which made her blush.

"Listen, Andy and I are starting a group. It's a *discussion group*, on Thursday nights. Would you guys want to join?"

Annabelle and Emily nodded, smiling. Christopher and Wallace moved over to join their conversation. "So what are we talking about?" Christopher asked.

There was a moment of silence, while Andy and Ben looked to Annabelle and Emily. Emily shook her head. She didn't want to endanger Wallace.

"Just wondering when the Lions are going to start playing again." said Ben.

"You're right! I hadn't thought about football, but since the war is over I wonder if they're going to have a team. It should be the Super Bowl in a couple weeks. Man, that's crazy."

"Kids, it's time for dinner, everyone take a seat at the table," Isabelle ushered them all over to the table, which had been moved out of the kitchen and into the living room. It was crammed with a mixture of stools and chairs, enough to accommodate the large dinner party in such a small room.

After they were seated, Michael raised his wine glass, "I'd like to make a toast. To all of us being here together. I'm so grateful that our guests could make it tonight and that we're here to host them."

They all raised their glasses, with Christopher adding, "Here, here, thanks, Dad!"

Emily looked across the table at her mother, who was smiling with tears in her eyes. She was obviously missing her father and Daniel.

"And to my mom, who has shown such strength and continues to guide us."

"Here, here!" added Wallace.

They all clinked glasses.

———

January 17, 2061

Emily stood at the white board in the front of her classroom. The new map of The Five would be projected onto the board, and her first lesson was to present the map to her students. There was a script explaining the restructuring she had been made to memorize during orientation, and she could take limited questions from the class; no more than two or three.

As the students filed in, Emily took a deep breath. She was about to teach about a world she did not believe in to a group of impressionable, bright eyed six and seven year olds. Most of them had no idea what the map had been before, and this was their introduction to their continent's geography.

"Please sit in your assigned seat. They are numbered, and they match the number you were given when you registered for school."

The children were each holding a number on a small index card to find their desks. One small girl, with her hair in a long braid down her back, came up to Emily and tugged on the end of her sweater sleeve. "I left my number on the bus. Can you please help me?"

Emily knelt down so she was eye level with the girl, "Yes, of course. What is your name?"

"Mei Ying Northrup."

Emily stood up and picked up her school-issued device from her desk. She scrolled through her attendance sheet until she got to Northrup. "You are number 19, dear."

Mei Ying nodded, "Thank you, Miss Caring," and headed toward desk 19.

Once they all were seated, Emily began the first lesson. "Hello class, and welcome to the first grade. I am your teacher, Miss Caring. This year we will be going on all sorts of adventures in the books we will read, the equations we will solve, and the languages we will explore, but first we're going to go over the maps of North America, and The Five. There's no need to take out your devices yet, just listen and then you can ask me some questions after I'm done."

Emily tapped her device. The lights dimmed in the classroom, and a map of North America before the war appeared on the screen. "What you see here is a map of North America, the continent on which we live, before the war. It was made up of three countries: Canada, the United States of America, and Mexico. The United States of America was made up of fifty individual states. You have a list of them in your devices and we will go over them later this week. For now, we're going to start with this state." Emily tapped her device and the map highlighted Michigan. "And this city," she tapped again and Detroit was highlighted.

A boy in the front raised his hand. He was at desk number 1. Emily pulled up the attendance list on her device and found his name.

"Yes, Jeffrey Martin, I will take questions at the end of the presentation."

"But Miss Caring, what's Michigan?"

Emily paused, taking a minute to process it and come up with an "appropriate" answer.

"It was one of the states in the United States of America. Detroit used to be its capital. Now, several of the old states came together to make the New Republic, and Detroit is the capital of that new country."

Jeffrey furrowed his brow, still visibly confused.

"Don't worry, Jeffrey, we'll go over the full list of states later on this week. This is just an overview of all the maps."

Jeffrey shrugged, and Emily continued. "So Detroit, this is the city where we live and where this school is. We are in Detroit now. When the Honorable General Huang decided to help the people here, give us freedom, and overthrow the government of Michigan, he did the right thing and his bravery inspired other states to become part of this freedom movement."

Emily tapped her device and Michigan lit up again, followed by the other states as she listed them, "First Minnesota said it wanted to be free too, and then Iowa, Indiana, and Ohio, and finally Illinois and Wisconsin. And that is how we became the New Republic."

Emily tapped her device, and the screen lit up the section of those former states as one block. The states' names disappeared and a new name lit up over them, "New Republic."

Several children raised their hands. "Wait, I'm not finished. I will take questions at the end. Okay, so it turned out Texas had wanted freedom for a long time too, so it declared itself its own country. That means General Huang's message reached them all the way down here," she tapped her device and Texas lit up, "and inspired them to be free."

"Now, the President of the United States, President Warren, did not like that. He does not believe in freedom. He wants to take money from the people so he can control them. He tried to use his military power to stop General Huang, but he failed because the military of the New Republic is strong and powerful. Only a few small states wanted to stay with President Warren, and those states became the United North." The states' names from the United North disappeared, and that block lit up with "United North" written over it.

"So then, another area of the country saw what the United North had done, and decided they wanted to become their own country too. These were the same states that had tried to become their own country two hundred years ago in the First Civil War, but they had failed. This time, they succeeded and became the Confederacy." The states' names from the Confederacy disappeared, and that block lit up with "Confederacy" written over it.

"After that happened, General Huang generously offered to join with the remaining states and make them part of the New Republic, but they decided to be their own country too. This was a mistake and they will probably join us soon, but for now they became Northwest America." The states' names from Northwest America disappeared, and that block lit up with "Northwest America."

"There were only two states left then, Alaska and Hawaii," Emily tapped her device and Alaska and Hawaii lit up. "Canada invaded Alaska and conquered it, so it's part of Canada now." Alaska lit up alone, and its name disappeared. Then Hawaii lit up alone. "And Hawaii used to be an independent kingdom, so its native people, like the people in the New Republic, decided they wanted to be free again and declared independence." The words "Kingdom of" appeared next to Hawaii. "General Huang admires this very much and we are friends with the Kingdom of Hawaii."

Emily tapped her device. The new map of North America (Canada, The Five, and Mexico) went up on the board, and each of the seven countries lit up in different colors to show their distinct borders.

"So this is the new map of North America. Thanks to General Huang, we can all live happily together now, in peace." Emily tapped her device one final time. The map disappeared and the lights came back up. "Okay, now do you have any questions?"

Every hand in the room went up.

_____

January 27, 2061

It was 9:00 pm, two hours before the government-mandated curfew. The first meeting was to be held in Ben's apartment. Since he lived in her building, Emily didn't have to worry about the curfew, but Andy and Annabelle did. She had told her mother that she and Ben had formed a book club, and her mother was delighted. Ben had passed his bar exam and his prospects were looking good. Annabelle had told her parents that Andy was helping her study. He had been an economics major too and she didn't want to fall behind. Her parents, especially her father, were very pleased.

"Okay, Mom, I'm heading down to Ben's."

Catherine looked up from her book and smiled at Emily. She was sitting on the couch in the living room. Wallace was out with Hillary. "Have a good time dear. Tell Ben I say hello."

"Will do," Emily leaned down to give her mother a hug.

When she rose up, she looked down at Catherine. She couldn't get over how much older she looked. She tried not to think about her father and Daniel, but she knew her mother was thinking about them all the time.

"Have a good night, Mom."

"Thanks, sweetheart, I will. I'm so glad that you're becoming friends with Ben. You don't even have to leave the building to see him."

Emily nodded and smiled, "Bye, Mom," then she turned and left.

———

Ben was in his apartment, humming a song he had loved before the war, when there was a knock at the door. He peered through the peephole. It was Annabelle and Andy. Ben swung open the door, "Hey guys, come in, come in."

"Wow man, I can't believe this place is so small. I mean you told me, but wow. We could have met at my place."

Ben chuckled, "No, we couldn't. Your place is further away and this way we aren't endangering the girls with the curfew. Annabelle just has to walk a couple blocks and Emily doesn't even have to leave the building." Just then there was another knock on the door. "Speak of the devil."

Ben looked through the peephole again and there she was, Emily Caring. "Come in, come in."

"Thanks," Emily smiled. "Hey guys."

"Hey, Em." Annabelle gave Emily a hug, and Andy waved.

Ben sat down in a chair by the bathroom, while Emily and Annabelle sat on the bed, and Andy on the floor.

"Okay, guys, I've checked my apartment and it's not bugged, and since we've all turned our devices off we should be safe." They all nodded. "Good. Well Andy and I wanted to start these meetings to discuss how we're going to shape the New Republic. General Huang has brought in martial law and I don't think it will last that long. People didn't fight for four years to end up repressed like this. They're going to want freedom, but without violence. And I think if we work hard enough, we can give it to them."

"That's some pretty big talk," said Annabelle.

Andy laughed, "Yes, yes it is. But it's the kind of talk that can get us out of this mess. We may never be the United States again, but we can at least make the New Republic the best of The Five."

"Thanks, Andy," Ben added. "Now I took the bar exam over a week ago and I should know my results next week. Once I've passed and I'm licensed, I'm going to try and get a job in the foreign affairs office. I speak Arabic fluently, and from what I understand, Huang is looking to open an embassy in Saudi Arabia, is that right?"

Andy nodded, "Yes, that's right. He wants to get arms and ammunition, to keep control, and keep the oil options open."

"But the U.S. hasn't traded with Saudi Arabia in twenty years," said Emily.

"Yes, exactly, we're not the U.S. This is the New Republic."

"So what you're saying is, you don't want the U.S. to get back together? You want to support this new, crazy government?"

"No, no. We don't want to support the government. We want to transform it from the inside out. Most people do. They don't want Huang in power. They want a country they can be proud of."

Emily nodded, "I get it. I do."

"Me too," Annabelle added.

Ben smiled, "Good. Now let's talk about your roles and who else we can recruit."

"Our roles? Wait a minute, slow down. I'm not ready to start a revolution tonight. I just started my internship. My family is just getting settled in. I thought we were going to talk about our issues with the new government, maybe reminisce about our lives before the war. Let's take this one step at a time," Annabelle said.

"Every minute we wait, is another minute they're in control," replied Ben.

"Okay, let's think about this logically," Emily spoke softly, making eye contact with Ben, Annabelle, and Andy one by one. "We don't want the government to stay, but we don't want it to leave either. We know that reuniting the United States is bigger than we can accomplish alone, and may not even be the right move, but we want the New Republic to be a better place to live in than it is now. Correct?"

Andy and Annabelle nodded.

"Okay then. I don't know a lot about politics but I know someone who does. I'm going to talk to my father."

Annabelle gasped.

"Wait, who's your father?" Andy asked.

"My father is John Caring, the former Attorney General of Michigan.

He's in the federal prison, awaiting trial."

Ben nodded, "That would be great Emily. Thank you."

"You're welcome. Until then, I agree with Annabelle. Who here knows who the current cabinet members are or how to get in touch with them? I don't even know when the first election is, do you?"

"It's in June. The government wants to prove that they earned their power. That they're not a dictatorship."

"Okay then, Ben, can you put together a list of cabinet members, upcoming elections, and open seats? Andy and Annabelle, find out everything you can about the current administration from where you work. Who's loyal, who's not. Start figuring out the politics of Detroit, now that it's the capital of the New Republic. And I'll make an appointment to see my father. He was as high up as you could get in Michigan and I'm sure he will be able to help, with information anyway."

Ben was smiling ear to ear, while Andy and Annabelle were nodding.

"Great, well now that we're all decided, Ben, seriously. How do you cook in this place?"

Everyone laughed, and Ben answered, "I eat a lot of microwave dinners."

"Well that has to stop. Feel free to come up and have dinner with my family any time. My Mom loves to cook and I know she would like to have you there."

"That would be great, thank you."

There was a pause, and then Annabelle said, "You know what I miss? Sunday night football."

Andy perked up, "Seriously?"

"Yes, I loved watching football. My Dad and my uncles all played in high school and college. My Mom would make a big meal, something easy like chili or lasagna, and we would put on our Patriots' jerseys and watch."

"You rooted for the Patriots?"

"Yeah, my Dad's from Boston."

For the next hour they all talked about other things they missed from before the war—favorite sports teams and television shows. By the time they were done it was 10:45 pm, fifteen minutes before curfew. Andy walked Annabelle home, Emily went back upstairs, and Ben fell down on his bed, excited for the future.

———

February 16, 2061

Emily walked up to the registration office in downtown Detroit. She had never been to this office before. In order to make an appointment to visit her father, she would have to fill out the appropriate paperwork. She would have come sooner but this was the first weekday that she had any free time, and the office was only open from 8 am – 4 pm. Thankfully, Emily didn't have to be at school until after lunch. Her class had an in-service day, when government personnel would come in for the first time to discuss their patriotism to the New Republic. Teachers were allowed to be absent that morning, and their classes would resume in the afternoon.

The registration office was a very large, grey building with high ceilings. Emily guessed it might have previously been a warehouse. The perimeter was lined with high countertops, like a bank, and there were two workers at terminals behind the counter, along the back wall. They were both male, dressed in military fatigues with black bands around their arms. As she approached the desk, the man on the left looked up and addressed her. "Can I help you?"

"Yes, I would like to fill out the paperwork to see an inmate in the federal penitentiary."

"Not all inmates are allowed visitors. What is the inmate's name and date of birth?"

Emily felt her stomach sink. "John Caring, January 11, 1997."

The man tapped on the screen in his terminal for several seconds, and then his eyes widened.

"No, this prisoner is not allowed visitors."

Emily took several breaths, deciding what to do next. Then she remembered Kyle, the guy she knew from high school who had talked to her on the way out of the refugee camp. He had told her to get in touch with him if she needed anything. She wasn't sure how much power he had, but she could at least ask him. He wasn't behind the desk today, clearly, and it would be too obvious if she asked for him. She would have to find him out of the office and ask him then.

She looked up at the man and nodded, "I understand, thank you."

As soon as she walked out of the building, she headed toward the bus stop and there he was, Kyle, waiting for the bus. She couldn't believe her luck. It was uncanny. He happened to look up as she approached the bus stop so she waved.

"Hey, I can't believe I ran into you. How are you?"

"I'm good, I'm good, just heading over to see my parents on my day off. They still live in the same house, but I'm in the barracks downtown. How are you? Visiting the registration office?"

"Yes, just checking on a few things," Emily paused, not knowing whether to ask him. Apparently, she paused too long because then Kyle looked at her, quizzically. "What?"

"I was wondering, and please don't feel obligated to do this, but I was just wondering. Is there any way I could see my father? I haven't seen him in more than four years and I'd really like to visit him in prison."

Kyle furrowed his brow, "I'm not sure that's possible. Is that what you were doing at the office?"

"Yes."

"I see. Well, I'm guessing they told you that he's not allowed to have visitors. He was a green list guy, very high up, and well... I don't know."

Emily nodded her head in agreement, "Yes, of course. I'm sorry I asked."

Kyle put his hand on her shoulder, "No, I'm not saying I can't help you. I'm just saying it won't be easy. We'll have to arrange it on a day when he's meeting with his attorney. You could act as the attorney's assistant, that I could get passed through."

"He has an attorney?"

"Of course he does. The New Republic assigned an attorney to represent him. He'll be given a fair trial."

Emily paused. The conviction in Kyle's voice struck her. He truly believed in the New Republic. She couldn't let that stop her from accepting his help though, he was her only option.

"Well that would be great, Kyle, if you could arrange that."

"Sure, not a problem, I'm glad to help. I know how important family is to you, to everyone. Let me get your contact info and I'll let you know when the meeting will be."

"Great! Thank you so much."

Emily and Kyle exchanged contact information on their devices, and a few minutes later a bus pulled up.

"Are you getting on this one, number 46?"

"No, I'm heading back to school so I'm taking the number 20."

"Gotcha, well don't worry, Emily, I'll be in touch." Kyle leaned down and gave Emily a hug, which she returned. He boarded the bus, and a few minutes later Emily's bus came. She still couldn't believe her luck. She had run into him at just the right time, and now she could report at the meeting tomorrow night that she would be meeting with her father soon. It was perfect.

––––––––

February 17, 2061

John Caring was crouched on the floor of his cell. His head hung low between his knees. He was having trouble breathing. His chest was tight and his thoughts were murky. Nothing made sense but he felt impending doom. He knew he was having another panic attack and the only way to get back to normal was to measure his breathing. He took a long inhale, counting to ten, then held his breath for three seconds, and exhaled for ten seconds. He repeated this breathing pattern until he felt well again. The attacks had started after he was moved to an isolation cell over a month ago.

After the civil war ended, when the New Republic was formally established and people were allowed to return and resettle, the prisoners had been moved around. Huang didn't want any former government officials congregating and plotting a rebellion. John had been moved into isolation then, and had suffered from several panic attacks, usually in the late afternoon or evening; after another day of solitude and hopelessness had taken its toll, his mind began to warp.

If they would only set a trial date, he would be able to see hope and light at the end of the tunnel.

Suddenly, the door to his cell opened and a guard barked at him. "Get up, Mr. Caring. You get thirty minutes outside today, by order of President Huang."

John blinked several times. He had been outside once since he had been put in isolation, during the first week, and it had been a mistake. After ten minutes, the head guard had come out and pulled him back inside. He stood up and followed the guard outside. The sun was bright and the yard was deserted.

"Is this just for today or will I get time outside again?"

"You'll get thirty minutes, twice a day, every day, until you go to trial."

"Thank you. Has a trial date been set yet?"

"No."

John nodded his head, then glanced up at the sky, took a deep breath and smiled.

———————

March 24, 2061

Ben was increasingly frustrated with how long everything was taking. The elections were in three months and Emily had yet to speak with her father. It was becoming clear that they needed his advice. The new government had several members from the old government in it, people John Caring had worked with for years. Ben had gotten a position in the interim Attorney General's office, through some of Andy's connections. Every day, he was in the capital building, learning more about the government—who was truly loyal to Huang and who wasn't, but he couldn't be sure. Ben had only been there a month, but John Caring knew this place inside and out. He was their only lead. No one else was close enough to them to share anything, and Annabelle hadn't told her mother what they were up to yet. She didn't want to endanger her family. To that end, their group hadn't expanded either. It was still just the four of them, meeting every Thursday, gathering and comparing information.

"It's been over a month and you haven't gotten a meeting with your father, I think we should look into other options. Andy, do you know anyone who could get her in?"

"Kyle will arrange the meeting, I know it."

"Well he already 'arranged' two meetings and then canceled them."

"No, the prison canceled them. Kyle said they're waiting to set a trial date before arranging another meeting with his attorney."

"Or so he said, he could be conspiring with them. What if you get there and he doesn't give you any time with your father but arrests you instead?"

"He wouldn't do that."

"How do you know?"

"Listen, if he didn't want to help me, he wouldn't. Why would he risk his job? It doesn't make any sense!"

"Well then when is the meeting?"

"I told you, they have to set a trial date. When they do, then I'll have the meeting."

"We don't have that kind of time!"

"All right, okay enough," Andy said. "Emily, if Kyle hasn't arranged the meeting by next week then we move forward without your father's help, we'll just do the best we can. Ben, does that work for you?"

"Sure."

"Great, and Emily? Annabelle?"

Annabelle nodded immediately but Emily hesitated. "I still think we should give him more time, but I'll wait until next week to decide."

"Okay then, so next week, if Emily hasn't met with her father or doesn't have a meeting arranged, we will talk about moving forward with the planning stages for Ben's role in the election."

Ben opened his mouth to say something but just then Emily's phone rang. It was Kyle. He always came at just the right time.

"Hello Kyle, how are you?" Emily paused. "Yes, Sunday at 9 am would be great. Yes, of course, I'll meet him outside the penitentiary at 8:30. Thank you very much." Emily smiled, and then looked at Ben who nodded in approval. "Well that's settled then, I'm meeting with my father at 9 am on Sunday."

———

After that night's meeting, Emily wasn't sure whether she should tell her mother about going to see her father. If she did, she would have to reveal the whole plan and Kyle's role in it. If she didn't and her mother found out later that she had, it would hurt her. And she didn't dare tell Wallace; she didn't want to get him involved at all.

When she got inside their apartment, her mother was in the kitchen making tea. She popped her head out when she heard the door open.

"So how was book club?"

"It was great, thanks. How was your night?"

"Oh you know, the usual, I watched the news and then read for a while."

Emily looked at her mother, who had been through so much already, and knew she couldn't tell her. She didn't want her to worry and if the meeting with her father did go well, she could always tell her after.

"That sounds nice," Emily gave her mother a hug and a kiss on the cheek. "I'm just going to go to bed. Is Wallace home?"

"Not yet, he should be home any minute. I'm going to wait and make sure he's in before curfew, and then I'll be going to bed too."

"Okay, goodnight, Mom."

"Goodnight, dear."

———

March 27, 2061

Emily was standing on the sidewalk across the street from the penitentiary, almost an hour early for her appointment. She had taken an earlier bus to ensure that she wasn't late. She was trying to remain calm but the anxiety and apprehension of seeing her father again was overwhelming. She couldn't just embrace him and be reunited; she needed to get information, and she wasn't visiting him as his daughter, but rather as his attorney's assistant. Kyle told her that her father was aware of the arrangement, and she was on the visitor registry only as the attorney's assistant, no name.

The minutes ticked by and eventually Emily began to cry, quietly at first and then in deep, heaving sobs. She went around the corner and into an alley so no one could see her. She didn't sit down because she didn't want to wrinkle her suit. How could she do it? Just go in and interview her father like she didn't know him? And everyone was counting on her to get information that could help them. She felt like she was choking on her pain. Coughing and then taking sharp breaths. She let the grief pour out of her until she felt empty.

After she had pulled herself together, she checked her device. It was 8:21 am. She took out her water bottle and splashed some water on her face, drying it with a napkin from her purse. She reapplied her makeup and then walked back to the penitentiary.

The attorney was waiting in front of the entrance. "Hello, Emily, I'm Mr. Roberts, your father's government-appointed attorney. I understand your desire to see your father and you're very lucky that you know Mr. Gaines. You've got a friend there, young lady." Mr. Roberts put a paternal hand on Emily's shoulder. She smiled and fought back more tears. "Now we'll go in together, go through security, and then we will be called in to speak with your father one at a time. I've arranged it that way so you'll have some time alone with him. Don't be afraid. Attorney-client privilege means that these meeting are not recorded. You can say whatever you want to him. You'll only have a few minutes though so don't waste them. Do you have any questions?"

"Yes, thank you, I just wonder, how long have you been working with my father?"

Mr. Roberts nodded, "Well over a year now, since he was brought to the penitentiary."

"Okay, thank you."

"So, let's go in then. Shall we?"

Emily nodded and followed Mr. Roberts into the penitentiary.

The next twenty minutes were a blur; there was the sign in process (in which Mr. Roberts signed for both of them), security check (where they and their possessions were scanned), and the oath they had to take before entering the waiting room ("I shall not, and will not, discuss anything with the prisoner which could undermine the New Republic.")

As planned, Mr. Roberts went in first. He was in there for over an hour, and then it was Emily's turn. When he walked out he looked pale and tired. He nodded at Emily, who stood up shakily and then went to the door to the meeting room and knocked. The door opened slowly and sitting at a small table, with a chair across from it, was her father.

What struck her first was how small he appeared. He was thin and there were dark bags under his eyes. His hair was graying in places and thinning in the front. He had always been the picture of robust health, and now he seemed physically and emotionally diminished.

When he saw her, his pale blue eyes lit up and he stood to his full height of six feet. He stuck his hand out to shake hers as the guard outside pushed a button and the door closed. She leaned in for the handshake, but once the door was closed his arms widened and he pulled her in for a hug. She could feel his ribs under his shirt.

He pulled back and held her at arms-length for a moment, surveying her. He smiled widely and then spoke. "We don't have much time. Sit, please sit down and tell me everything or whatever it is you came here to say."

Emotion had surged up in Emily. She found it hard to breathe, let alone speak. Her eyes were welling up with tears and she had to take a sharp inhale and clear her throat before she could sit. Her father was seated now, looking up at her expectantly. She took her seat and began.

"Mother and Wallace are fine. We all live together in government housing. Daniel is still missing. No one will tell us anything. I didn't tell them I was coming to see you. I'm here actually because..." at this she paused, suddenly feeling guilty at coming to see her father because she wanted something; she couldn't think about that now. She had to get right to the point. "I'm here because I need your advice."

John Caring reached over and grasped Emily's hand and nodded.

"Okay, Dad, here's the thing. I've become friends with this group of people, well there's only four of us, including me, but one of them, well one of us, he wants to run for public office but we're not sure who in the government actually is with the revolution and who isn't or could easily be turned."

He stared at her for a moment and released her hand. "I see. So you're planning a coup d'état?"

"No, I mean not really. Not like before. We want to change things from the inside, not overthrow the government entirely. We want to make the New Republic the best of The Five. Make it fair and equitable."

"Emily, you know how dangerous this is. You understand the risks."

"Yes, sir."

"And you understand that you may not like everything I'm going to say. This isn't some debate over the dinner table or in school. This is real and some of these people are ruthless."

"Yes, sir." Emily could see the glint in her father's eye, his expert mind at word. Despite everything he had been through, he was still John Caring.

"All right then, let's begin. I assume you brought something to take notes with?"

Emily nodded, pulling out her device. It was a 6 x 9 tablet, an older, refurbished model she had gotten in the refugee camp.

Her father went on to detail everything he knew about the men and women in power in the New Republic, both before and after the war. The atrocities they had committed, people they had tortured and even killed. These were people she knew, people she had grown up around who had worked with her father. It was unreal. Her father went quickly, naming people by last name and correcting her notes when he saw she had gotten something wrong. All of a sudden a red light by the door started flashing.

"We're almost out of time," her father said. "Save that as a secure file and put away your device."

"Yes, of course." Emily stowed her device in her purse and stood up right as the door opened.

She smiled and shook her father's hand, "Good bye, Mr. Caring. It was a pleasure meeting you, and Mr. Roberts will be in touch."

"Thank you."

Two words; that was all her father said before a guard came in and took him away.

March 31, 2061

"So did he say who is the most influential?" Ben was sitting on the edge of his bed while Emily was recounting the information her father had given her. Though she had gone through security when leaving the prison, they only checked for weapons. Her device had not been scanned. Just like Kyle said.

"He listed four people he knew in the current administration whom he thinks are not actually with General Huang. Everyone else he either doesn't know personally or he isn't sure about. We have to keep in mind, which he stressed also, that he hasn't seen these people in years. We can't know for sure what their true feelings are based on his feelings about them."

"Sure, sure but he worked with them, he was in prison with at least one of them right?"

"Yes, the interim Attorney General was his Assistant Attorney General before the war, Isaac Rosenthal. He's running for a seat on the leadership council in June and he thinks that he's not really loyal to Huang. When they were first arrested, when the revolution started, he thinks Rosenthal made a deal. He can't be sure but he thinks so. He was released and my father wasn't."

"Seriously? I work for Attorney General Rosenthal. I'm in his department every day."

"I know you are."

"The guy is loyal to Huang. That's for sure. Why does your father think that?"

"Just wait, my father thinks he made the deal as a ruse. Rosenthal was a good guy and he believed in the United States. My father doesn't think he would betray his country. He thinks, and this is all speculation, but he thinks that perhaps Rosenthal laid low during the war and could be planning a coup. Well, actually, what he said was that if anyone from the old administration could plan it, Rosenthal could. And lots of people have a reason to."

Ben nodded, "So who else did he name?"

"A couple lower level officials, I wrote their names down… he said they wouldn't be very useful though," Emily leaned down and pulled out her device.

"Philip Gonzales and Joe Warshawsky but they moved abroad right before the war, and…" at this she paused and look up at Annabelle, "Annabelle's dad, Michael Stevenson. He said that before the war there was talk of some project he had been working on and when he asked me about him, I told him how he had been brought back from Canada and promoted. He said he didn't doubt his loyalty at all but whatever he's doing, it's not what's in his job description."

"What is that supposed to mean?" Annabelle asked curtly.

"No, don't misunderstand. He thinks your father is loyal, but whatever he's working on is very important to General Huang, and lucrative."

"So you're saying my father knows that what he's building could be good for Huang? Is that what you're saying?"

"No, I'm not accusing your father of anything and neither is my father. He's just saying we need to be careful."

Annabelle nodded, still visibly disturbed, "Okay."

"So how should we move forward?" Andy asked.

"I think we should side with Rosenthal. Work on his campaign. Get closer to him and his team," Ben responded confidently.

Emily nodded in agreement, "Yes, me too. Annabelle? Andy?"

They agreed in unison.

"Okay then, we'll side with Rosenthal, work on his campaign and see what we can find out. Let's talk about next steps, next week."

Annabelle looked at her watch, "Great, well, it's 10:45 so we should go."

"Right, okay, see you guys next week. Emily, can you stick around for a while?"

Emily looked at Ben quizzically, but agreed, "Sure."

After Annabelle and Andy had left, Ben turned to Emily.

"So Emily, listen. I know how hard it must have been to see your father under these conditions. And I know how hard I pushed you to get the information. I know I've been impatient and I just want to apologize, and say thank you."

Ben then put his hand on Emily's knee. It filled her with warmth and she started to blush. She pulled her hair behind her ears and leaned in closer to him. "I met your father, once, at the beginning of the revolution."

Emily pulled back, "What? You never told me that."

"It was very brief. I had been captured by the rebels and he was in the same group of prisoners. I was with him for less than a day. We barely spoke."

"You were rescued, and you left him there?"

"I didn't even know him. I didn't know who he was. I had only just met you the night before and you told me your name was Emily Johnson."

Emily nodded, "Yes, of course. How could you have known? I'm sorry."

"There's no need to apologize. All I wanted to say was that when I think about our cause, and you, I think about that man I met when I was a prisoner of the rebels. I think he's innocent, I do."

Emily smiled and reached for Ben's hand.

Just then there was a pounding on the door, three large thuds and then it burst off its hinges. Three men were standing there, all in army fatigues and black arm bands. One of them was Kyle.

"We're here for Emily Caring. Please identify yourself."

Emily stood up and slipped her device under the pillow on Ben's bed. "I'm Emily Caring."

Ben stood up too. "I'm Benjamin Hughes. What are you doing here?"

One of the soldiers moved forward, grabbing Emily's arm and handcuffing her hands behind her back, as Kyle pulled out his device and read from it aloud.

"Emily Caring, you are under arrest for treason. The New Republic has evidence that you have been conspiring with your father, John Caring, to overthrow the government."

Emily was dumbfounded. She thought she could trust Kyle. Ben was breathing heavily; visibly angry.

Kyle continued, "You have the right to remain silent. Anything you say can and will be used against you in a court of law. You have the right to an attorney. If you cannot afford an attorney, one will be provided for you."

Emily turned to Ben as she left with the soldiers, "Tell my mother what happened. That I've been arrested."

"Ms. Caring's family will be informed of her arrest," Kyle said curtly.

After they left, Ben wanted to call Andy and Annabelle to warn them but he couldn't. Their devices could be bugged. That's why they turned them off in their meetings.

He sat down on his bed and slid his hands back behind him. His left hand hit something under his pillow. He pulled it out. It was Emily's device. He smiled to himself; she was so smart.

The next day he would go to their office and tell Andy and Annabelle what had happened, but first he had to go upstairs and tell Catherine and Wallace.

———

April 1, 2061

It was 9:00 am. Ben was approaching the Department of the Interior. He had been up half the night comforting Catherine Caring, while Wallace paced back and forth in the living room. He couldn't imagine going through what she had; losing one son, her husband in prison, finally reuniting with her daughter only to have her get arrested a few months later.

Right after Emily left, Ben had used a scrambler program he had bought on the black market to encrypt everything on Emily's tablet. Only he had the key code to unscramble it.

He had almost reached the door to the Department of the Interior building when, out of nowhere, Kyle appeared from behind the trees which lined the entrance.

"Hello, Mr. Hughes. I figured you would be coming here this morning, to tell your friends about Ms. Caring's arrest last night."

Ben didn't say anything. He just eyed Kyle.

"You can tell them but I would advise against any sudden action. The government is watching you too, and any evidence we have that the three of you have been conspiring with John and Emily Caring could lead to your arrest."

"I thought you were her friend."

"I am her friend, but I'm an officer of the New Republic first. She'll get a fair trial, just like her father will."

"A trial? She's going to be put on trial? That's ludicrous."

"Even saying that could get you arrested. I'm trying to help you. Don't go in *there*, a government building, and say something that you'll regret."

Ben nodded. He wasn't sure how to read Kyle. He knew he couldn't be trusted, but there was something about him. Kyle clearly thought he was doing the right thing, the moral thing, by arresting Emily.

"Okay then. I'm heading back to the station." Kyle left, and Ben stood there for several minutes, contemplating his next move. Eventually, he turned around and went home. He needed more time to think about the future, and whether fighting this new government was worth it.

Life in the New Republic: Part II

Isaac Rosenthal was tall and broad. He had black curly hair and deep brown eyes. He had just celebrated his fifty-fifth birthday, but easily looked ten years younger. Isaac was a widower. His wife had been killed during the first few days of the revolution by a bomb set off in an empty train station. She was visiting her sister up north and had been hit by shrapnel while walking across the street. It was listed as an "incidental death" in the record of casualties; not by accident but not on purpose. They didn't have any children, his parents had died six years ago, and he didn't have any siblings. He was alone, which gave him a lot of time to think.

Isaac had not been in the capital when General Huang's forces arrived. He had been out on leave, grieving his wife, and it was his first day back. After his initial arrest and imprisonment he had been given a choice: join the revolution or remain in prison. He was considered a valuable asset due to his legal expertise. It was then that he made a different choice; he would join the revolution and after the dust settled he would find a way to take back the government. In the meantime, he would have to do things that went against his character, and he would have to say things he didn't mean.

Over the past four years, he had written more than half of General Huang's Proclamations to the Public, and he had helped draft the New Republic's Constitution. He drew the line at violence though. Luckily, as an attorney and not a soldier, he had only been in those situations twice and both times he was able to avoid it. This had been during the first year of the revolution.

The first time he had been at his desk, drafting a letter from General Huang to U.S. President Warren. People were rushing past his office. He stood up and began walking toward the door. That's when he saw a woman in plain clothes pointing a gun at him from across the aisle. "Stop!" she shouted. He instinctively raised his hands above his head. She moved toward him.

Then someone in a black ski mask ran up to her and grabbed her arm. "Don't waste your time with him. We have to get to the General!" And they left. That was the first assassination attempt of General Huang. There had been two since then and none had been successful.

The second time it was to travel with General Huang to see new prisoners from the green list. The General liked to do certain executions himself and sometimes he would call on those in his inner circle to take part. Isaac knew this, so he had stayed home from work that day, feigning the flu.

There were times during the war when he felt like he couldn't continue, especially during the first year. Then there had been a turning point. He had seen the plans for the Ultimate Ending Project. That's when he started secretly copying files and creating an archive at home. He had to know how the war would play out before he waged his own.

———

April 5, 2061

Wallace Caring was almost twenty years old. He was born on May 15, 2041. Since his sister Emily's arrest, he had been spending a lot of time at the public library, reading. Hillary had unceremoniously dumped him for another guy, and since then he had thrown himself into his school work. After leaving the library, he would take long walks along the Detroit River, but he was always home by curfew. Wallace felt lost.

During the war, he had been a comfort to his mother. Being separated from the rest of their family, he knew he had to survive for her. After the war, when they were housed with Emily, he thought things would start to be normal again. Then, almost a month ago, he had been walking home, on his way back from a date with Hillary, when he saw his mother getting out of a car two blocks from their apartment building. The driver was a man; he recognized him but couldn't place him at first. As the car pulled away the expression on his mother's face startled him. It was warm, loving. He waited until she was in the apartment building before continuing his walk, so he would enter after her. As far as he knew, his mother's only friends were Mr. and Mrs. Stevenson, Annabelle and Christopher's parents.

When he entered the apartment, his mother was in the kitchen, humming and making a cup of tea. She looked up when she saw him and smiled. "Hi, dear, how was your day?"

"It was good, thanks, Mom. How was yours?" Something told Wallace not to ask her about the man in the car, just to wait and see what she said, if she mentioned it.

"It was nice. I had lunch with Isabelle, then came home and did some reading." She was lying, or at least omitting.

"So you've been home since lunch?"

At this Catherine paused for a moment then replied, "Yes, of course. That's what I said. Why? Is something wrong?"

"No, I just thought you had other plans; that's all."

"Oh, no, dear, I didn't. Maybe you're thinking of tomorrow when I'm volunteering at the school?"

"Yes, that must have been it."

"Well dinner is almost ready, you go wash up and I'll set the table."

Wallace went to the bathroom to wash his hands. Was his mother having an affair? He shook his head. No, that was impossible. She was too old.

———

April 7, 2061

Ben had thought long and hard about his next move. He could go home to Beirut, and forget about the New Republic, or he could take the job his father had arranged for him in the United North. Something told him not to choose either option. Whatever Huang had Annabelle's father, Michael Stevenson, working on was big enough to impact the rest of the world. He had to stay and do what he could to stop it.

If Emily's father, John Caring, was right about Isaac Rosenthal, then they were here for the same reason. Both he and Rosenthal wanted to change the New Republic from within and stop Huang from maintaining power, and the election was coming up for the cabinet.

Huang's position was not on the ballot, but several others were, and Rosenthal was running for Attorney General, second in command under the new Constitution. As a Huang insider, it was all but guaranteed that he would win. And if John Caring was right, that could change everything.

How was Ben supposed to approach him though? What if John Caring was wrong? The only person he knew who knew Isaac Rosenthal, and was safe to approach, was Catherine Caring. So that was where he would begin. He had only interacted with her briefly before Emily's arrest, casual pleasantries in the lobby and the one dinner at the Stevenson's. After the last time though, when he had told her about Emily's arrest, they had talked for a long time and he hoped she would trust him enough to help him.

———

Catherine was sitting across from Ben in her living room. Wallace was out, again. It was 8:00 pm. She was remembering the first time she had seen Ben and the way her daughter had reacted. She understood why Emily had developed feelings for him. He had kind eyes and a noble face. There was an earnestness to the way he spoke that conveyed a sense of purpose. He honestly believed he was working for a greater good.

Ben leaned forward slightly. "Thank you for meeting with me. I really appreciate it."

Catherine nodded. "What is this about? Have you heard anything about Emily? I'd like to visit her."

Ben shook his head. "Unfortunately that won't be possible for the time being. She's still in isolation; no one can see her until a hearing

144

date is set... and that could take weeks, even months."

"Months?"

"I'm so sorry."

There was a pause. Catherine was holding a small cloth in her hands, rolling it back and forth, tying it and untying it. Her nerves were building. "So what is it you came to talk to me about then, if it's not about Emily?"

"I came to talk about Isaac Rosenthal."

Catherine leaned forward. "Isaac? Why?"

"Well when Emily went to see your husband, he told her that if anyone in Huang's administration wasn't truly loyal, it was Mr. Rosenthal."

Catherine nodded.

"Okay, well I was hoping you could corroborate that in some way, before I approach him."

"Why would you want to approach him?"

Ben was confused. Given all that had happened he figured that she would understand his motives. "If he really does want to undermine Huang's government, then he's on our side. I could work with him on the inside; help remove Huang from power, free political prisoners, including Emily and your husband."

Catherine leaned back. "I see."

"I'm sorry I didn't think this was a sensitive subject. I apologize.

I was just hoping, since you knew Rosenthal and everything, that maybe you would have some insight into his true loyalties?"

"I do know Isaac Rosenthal, quite well. We were having an affair until his wife died."

Ben was stunned. Until now, he had seen Catherine Caring as a grieving wife and mother, the idea of her having an extramarital affair would never have occurred to him.

Catherine continued, "I can tell you, beyond a shadow of a doubt, that he is not loyal to General Huang or his dictatorial regime."

"Have you been in contact with him?"

"Yes."

"Since the war was over? Since you've lived here?"

"Yes."

"So you know what he's planning?"

Catherine shook her head. "I don't know what he's planning, exactly, but I do know that he plans to overthrow Huang."

"Do you think, I mean, would you feel comfortable, arranging a meeting?"

"I can ask him, but Ben, what you're doing... you'll be no help to Emily or to your cause if you get arrested too."

"I know. I understand. I need to try to get to the inside of Huang's government though."

Catherine nodded. "Yes, well. I'm not sure if Isaac will even meet with you, but I'll ask."

"Thank you. How are you doing, overall?"

"It's okay, Ben, I know you have other things to do."

"No, really, I want to know. I had no idea that you were... well that you had other... friends, outside of your family I mean."

At this Catherine laughed, "Yes, well. My relationship with Isaac is not exactly something I'm proud of, or that I broadcast. And my children don't know, of course. I assume I can trust you."

"Yes, of course."

"Anyway, I'm fine. Thank you for asking. This war continues to takes its toll on us, on everyone. At least I have Wallace."

"Yes, where is Wallace?"

"He's at the library, studying. He should be home any minute. He's been studying late recently, so we've been having dinner at 8 or 8:30 pm; would you like to stay for dinner? I made lasagna."

"Yes, that would be great, thank you."

Over the next hour, until Wallace came home, Ben learned a lot about Catherine Caring and her relationship with Isaac Rosenthal. The affair had lasted two years, before the war. John Caring had been distant and increasingly spending more time at the office. He had changed in other ways too. His moral compass had changed, and he had participated in discussions about repressing the rebels that Catherine hadn't thought possible of him ten or even five years before. He had shown a calculated indifference to human suffering.

Then she revealed something that was so telling, Ben repeated it to himself for days after.

"The methods used during the war, the fact that Emily is in prison now, is not what I ever wanted, and I understand why people revolted. I saw how they were living, what the government was doing, and I understand why people rose up against my husband and that administration."

Once Wallace came home, their conversation came to an abrupt halt. There were some things Catherine was not ready to share with her children, especially about their father.

———

April 11, 2061

Catherine had arranged for Ben to have a meeting with Rosenthal at his office in the capital building. Rosenthal's theory was that hiding in plain sight was best. His schedule was so busy that if he was seen venturing too far afield to meet with someone in his own department, someone he could meet with whenever he wanted, it could arouse suspicion.

Ben was sitting outside of his office. Rosenthal's assistant, Jonathan, was behind a desk, typing. His phone rang. Jonathan nodded saying, "Yes, sir," and hung up the phone. Then he looked up at Ben. "Mr. Rosenthal will see you now."

Ben stood up quickly, saying, "Thank you" as he walked up to the office door and knocked.

"Come in."

Rosenthal's office was spacious, impressive. There were two large windows at the back, behind his desk. Several framed paintings lined the left wall, and there was a row of bookshelves along the right wall. Rosenthal was standing by the bookshelves and strode over to shake Ben's hand as he entered.

Ben closed the door behind him, then turned and shook hands with him.

Rosenthal motioned for Ben to follow him, "Please, sit down."

Ben sat down in one of the chairs across from the desk, while Rosenthal sat behind his desk.

"So, Catherine told me you wanted to talk about John Caring?"

Ben wasn't sure what to say next. How much did Rosenthal know? "Umm yes, well, about his beliefs, mostly."

"I see. John was a good man but he made some bad choices, some pretty bad decisions."

Ben nodded, not knowing how to proceed. Rosenthal said nothing. "Well, yes. I see how it could be interpreted that way..." Ben took a deep breath then continued, "Mr. Rosenthal, sir. When Emily met with Mr. Caring, he said you might share some of his beliefs, perhaps. That you believed in justice in a deeper way than the new government does."

Rosenthal leaned forward. "What are you implying?" This was it. Rosenthal was testing him.

"I believe you may have a plan to overthrow General Huang and take control of the government."

"There we are. Mr. Hughes if you want to work with me, as Catherine says you do, then we need to be honest with each other. If at any time you are dishonest or betray me in any way, I won't hesitate to take retaliatory action. Do you understand?"

Ben smiled. "Yes, sir."

"Good. Well then, I'm going to promote you. It may take a couple weeks, but I'm going to make you my new assistant."

"What about Jonathan?"

"Oh he never wanted to be anyone's assistant. He's been hinting at a transfer since he got here. He couldn't apply for one, of course, until he'd been in the position over a year, but I'll approve it now. You will be his replacement, but more than that. With your law degree, I'll need you to be an assistant counsel. I'll hire a new secretary from the applicant pool to work for both of us."

Ben's eyes lit up. This was the very position he had hoped for. "Very good, thank you, sir."

"I've reviewed your resume, and gotten some background information from Catherine. I'm curious, why did you come to Detroit? You could have stayed in Lebanon or gone anywhere really. Why here?"

"That's a good question. And it's one I've asked myself several times, both before I left Beirut and since I've been back. There's something about this place. I was born just outside Detroit, in Bloomfield Hills. My parents are both from there. We moved to Beirut when I was three, but we always came back here to visit family. I felt like in Lebanon I was "the American kid" and when I came back here I was an outsider too. When I came back to do my mandatory year, something just clicked. I knew I wanted to come back, to come 'home.' And then after I graduated, I was interviewing for jobs when the revolution started. I was captured by the revolutionaries. My father rescued me and I spent the last few years in Lebanon, but I couldn't let these people take over my home... the one place where I felt like I belonged. So I came back, to change that."

Rosenthal nodded. "I respect that Mr. Hughes and I understand it." Then he stood up and reached his hand out, Ben shook it. "I'm very glad you approached Catherine the way you did, and I look forward to working together. I'll arrange your promotion by the end of the week."

"Thank you, sir."

And that he did. By Thursday, Jonathan had been moved to another department and Ben was Isaac Rosenthal's assistant counsel.

———

From then on, Ben arranged Rosenthal's schedule and was included in some of his meetings, taking diligent notes. Rosenthal was a master politician. He carefully avoided certain situations while taking full advantage of others. His alliances ran the gamut, overlapping at times with those in power whom he claimed to despise, but he continued to be above suspicion due to his expert maneuvering.

Sometimes Ben would get lost, not knowing the end game of a certain relationship or how different alliances played into Rosenthal's strategy. They would then stay late while Rosenthal explained. Neither of them knew the full details of the Ultimate Ending Project, and Rosenthal hadn't yet shared his home archive of information with Ben. He hadn't shown anyone that, not even Catherine. That information was far too sensitive. It was getting to the time when he had to tell Ben though. The election was close and he needed to have all the information. It wasn't an easy thing to discuss since it involved Michael Stevenson and Rosenthal knew that Ben was close with Stevenson's daughter, Annabelle. He decided to ask him about it one day, when they were working late on a draft of an upcoming speech for General Huang.

"So, how well do you know Annabelle Stevenson?"

Ben had been waiting for this question. He had hesitated to bring up the Stevensons because of the sensitivity of Mr. Stevenson's job, but now he supposed was the time.

"Pretty well, I guess. We used to have those weekly meetings, as I told you, with Andy too. After Emily's arrest we stopped for a while. They both know that I'm working here now and that was part of our plan. You know all that though."

"I'm more asking if you know her personally... or her family well?"

"No, we're not involved romantically and I've only met her parents once, at a dinner party, several months ago."

"I see."

"Why? What is it?"

"I think it's time for me to explain the Ultimate Ending Project to you. Michael Stevenson is the head engineer and if it comes to it, we may have to get him out of the way."

———

June 1, 2061

When Emily first got to prison, she had gone through a registration process. There was the official process, where her clothes and belongings were confiscated, and there was the unofficial process conducted by the male security guards. They considered it their own private initiation process for female inmates to keep them in line in the future.

After being strip searched by a female guard, Emily had been taken to the showers to wash before being issued her prison uniform. It was there that they had gotten her. The showers were in a long hallway. The floor was tiled and there were three drains in the center of the floor. The steam was so thick she could hardly see. The water was scalding hot. As she walked quickly into the hallway she felt a hand reach out and grab her buttocks. She screamed and started to run when a large man stepped out of the shadows. He was clothed from the waist down but soaking wet. She was afraid to look up at him. He grabbed her arms, picking her up and forcing her against the wall. He was laughing. She screamed for him to stop, writhing beneath his grip. He covered her mouth to silence her, and then turned her around so her chest hit the wall, hard. He jammed his fingers inside her, first her vagina and then her anus. Then another man grabbed her arm and yanked her out from under the first man. He was smaller than the other man, but still out-weighed her by forty pounds.

"Want to dance, princess?" His breath reeked of vodka.

He hoisted her over his shoulder, spanking her buttocks and kicking water in the air with his combat boots. Eventually he let her go and her body fell to the floor. Then someone kicked her stomach, hard.

"Get up!" barked a voice above. "Get up, get out of here, and get dressed!"

Emily crawled to the end of the hallway. She stood up slowly, her body shaking. The door at the end of the hallway opened and she was ushered into a small room with fluorescent lighting. A female guard wrapped a towel around her. Emily started to cry but bit her lip. She didn't know what was in store for her next and she didn't want to show any vulnerability. Living in the refugee camp had hardened her and made her aware of what people were capable of if given the opportunity. If they thought you were weak, they would take advantage of you.

The female guard rubbed the towel over her back, mumbling, "It looks like they didn't get you too bad, probably because you're Mr. Caring's daughter... didn't want to take any chances."

Emily looked at her with confusion. The guard handed her a faded army green jumpsuit and a pair of black sandals.

"Here you go. Laundry is done on Thursdays. You'll get one of these a week."

Emily nodded, put on the jumpsuit and sandals, and shuffled out of the room.

That was two months ago, since then she had been in solitary confinement. She was limited to two walks outside per day, thirty minutes each.

———

June 15, 2061

Rosenthal and Ben were in Rosenthal's apartment. It was sparse, almost Spartan. There were no pictures on the walls or in frames anywhere in the living room. All of those things had gone into boxes after his wife died and he had moved out of their house and into this apartment. There was a vase of flowers on a table in the kitchen that Catherine had given him. The flowers were almost dead. She brought flowers when she came by once or twice a week, depending on his schedule.

It was comforting to be with her but it never made him feel any less alone. His relationship with Catherine had been a way to escape his troubled marriage, and after his wife died and the revolution started they couldn't continue it. Now that they were seeing each other again he realized that's all it ever was and was ever going to be. Something comforting to hold onto in the darkness, but not something that brought in the light.

Rosenthal went to the bookcase in the corner of the living room. He took several books off of the top shelf and then removed the panel behind it. Behind the panel was a box. He took it out and put it on the coffee table, next to the couch.

He motioned to Ben, "Open it."

Ben sat down on the couch and took off the top of the box. Inside were stacks of papers; most were copies of blueprints. He pulled out the papers and noticed they were numbered with colored tabs at the top. Rosenthal took the papers from Ben and stacked them next to the coffee table.

"This is what Stevenson and Huang are working on. It's called the Ultimate Ending Project."

Rosenthal took number ten and unfolded it. It was a large document, so he spread it out over the entire table top. Half of the document was a blueprint, pieced together using four photographs; the second half was a bullet-pointed list. Rosenthal ran his index finger over the blueprint.

"This is a hydraulic bomb; it's very small, about the size of an apple. It can be made at various concentrations, but at its most intense, if it's completed, it would be more powerful than any nuclear or atomic bomb the world has ever seen." He moved his finger over to the list. "And this is how to detonate it."

Ben was frozen, just staring at the paper as Rosenthal read the detonation instructions aloud. There's no way Annabelle's father could be building this. That would be insane, but here he was, looking at the blueprints and the instructions.

When Rosenthal finished, he paused. "I know what you're thinking and yes, Stevenson knows what he's building."

Ben took a deep breath and finally spoke, "Okay, so what are we going to do about it?"

"We need to create a plan to dismantle this program whether or not we win the election."

"But how?"

"We need to get to Michael Stevenson."

Ben nodded. "I see. And this is where I come in?"

"Yes, yes it is."

"The election is two weeks away. Are you sure you want me getting involved in this, now?"

"Now is the only time. Earlier it would have given Stevenson time to find a way out before the election, too much later and it's the same scenario. It has to be now."

———

June 17, 2061

Ben was nervous. He didn't know what Mr. Stevenson would do when he approached him. Andy and Annabelle had been dating for a couple months, so Andy was at the Stevensons' apartment at least once a week. He knew when Mr. Stevenson was usually home, and Andy had checked with Annabelle to be certain. Rosenthal was right; they couldn't talk to Stevenson at his office. Even with all the power Rosenthal had in the government, the Ultimate Ending Project was too serious. And given Stevenson's expertise in the area, and his value to Huang, they couldn't risk just eliminating him outright. They had to be cautious, but yet forthright. A delicate balance Ben had seen his father manage as a diplomat his entire life.

He and Andy walked up to the front door of the apartment.

"You ready?" Andy asked.

Ben nodded.

Andy knocked and Annabelle answered the door. She reached up and gave him a hug and a kiss on the cheek.

"Hey Ben," she said.

They both walked into the apartment. Mr. Stevenson was seated in the living room, reading.

He looked up when they entered the room.

"Hello, boys."

Andy nodded at Annabelle and they both retreated to her room. Ben walked to the chair across from where Mr. Stevenson was seated and sat down.

Mr. Stevenson put his newspaper down and sat up. "Well hello, Ben. Is there something I can help you with?"

Ben was becoming more nervous. His heart rate quickened. "Yes, Mr. Stevenson. I wanted to ask you something."

"Well all right, of course, what is it?"

Ben began, "Emily, before she was arrested, she went to the prison to see her father."

"Now let me stop you right there. I won't talk about any of that stuff with John and Emily Caring. You know I work for this government and I won't compromise that. Well you know that better than anyone, you work for the Attorney General."

"He's the interim Attorney General actually. It won't be official until after the election."

Mr. Stevenson nodded. "That may be the case, but either way you know we're not to be discussing this; any prisoners, as a matter of fact."

"Yes, I understand, and of course I respect your position."

"Our position—we both work for the same government."

"Yes, sir, but this isn't about John or Emily Caring. I have a question about you."

Mr. Stevenson crossed his arms over his chest. "What?"

"When Emily visited John Caring in prison, he told her that you might be working on something very important for Huang. Something called the Ultimate Ending Project."

"That's enough now, Ben, you can't just come into my house like this and..."

Ben interrupted him, "I'm so sorry Mr. Stevenson. It's just that I don't think you understand the implications of this, of the project. I'm trying to understand your thought process."

Stevenson leaned forward, whispering, "I don't know how you even know about the project, but even discussing it with you is treasonous... wait, did Rosenthal put you up to this?"

"Look, it doesn't matter how I know..."

"Yes, it does."

Ben sat up straight and looked Stevenson in the eye. He wasn't a kid anymore, he was a man fighting to save his country from ruin. "With all due respect, sir, you and I both know that Huang will not stay in power forever. Things have started to settle down since the revolution, and the people are looking for a more even approach. That will be reflected in the coming election. The project you're working on can't get into the wrong hands if the election doesn't go Huang's way. Please, sir. Come to Rosenthal's office tomorrow to discuss this."

Mr. Stevenson paused, eyeing Ben. Slowly he nodded, "I knew it was Rosenthal. Okay then, I'll be there."

Ben smiled. "Thank you, sir."

_____

June 18, 2061

"Where is he?"

"He will come."

Rosenthal was pacing in his office, waiting for Stevenson to arrive. It was 10:00 am on Saturday. The election was a week from Tuesday. There was a knock at the door.

"Come in."

Michael and Isabelle Stevenson entered.

"Hello, Mr. and Mrs. Stevenson, we weren't expecting you both," Ben said.

"Yes, well. If I'm going to work with you, then Isabelle has to know all that's going on. She knows as much, if not more, about the project as I do. She worked on it in its original form in graduate school. She's an expert in re-harnessing emissions and turning them into clean energy."

"The project is fueled by clean energy? I thought it was nuclear?"

"No, it's not," Isabelle said, stepping forward.

"General Huang is committed to building our defenses without nuclear engagement. He doesn't want to go that route. Though his methods may seem brutal, it's nothing compared to what the United States did in the past, and what other countries are doing now. Look at China!"

Rosenthal nodded, "Yes, I understand why, as a scientist, you feel that way."

"There's no need to be insulting."

"I'm not, honestly. From looking at the blueprints I assumed it was nuclear. If you've found a way to harness emissions, turn them into clean energy, and weaponize them, that's very impressive. You're wrong about Huang though. I know him better than anyone in this room, if he remains in power he will use them to expand his... influence."

"The project isn't a weapon!" Isabelle exclaimed.

"All due respect, I'm an engineer. I've seen the blueprints, it's a weapon," Ben said. "And it's called the Ultimate Ending Project."

"An end to climate change, not to life," said Isabelle. "What do you mean you've seen the blueprint? How did you get access?"

"I've been monitoring this project since the beginning of the revolution," said Rosenthal.

"You mean there was someone working on this while we were in Canada?" asked Michael.

"Yes, two scientists worked on it intermittently during the war. When they couldn't get far enough along, Huang had them killed.

That's why he brought you back, to work on it again," replied Rosenthal.

"Then why not hire Isabelle?"

"I'm not sure."

"We only came back so that we could monitor the project, make sure it didn't get into the wrong hands and get weaponized."

"And you think working on it for Huang was the putting it in the right hands?" Ben questioned.

"He already had the work we had done before the war, and we decided that if we were here to monitor it, we could stop it from being used incorrectly. Very few people understand the science as well as we do; in fact, I don't know anyone who knows it as well as Isabelle."

Rosenthal nodded. "So what are you going to do with it now?"

"What do you want us to do? Why did you ask me to come here?" asked Michael Stevenson.

"The election is in less than two weeks. We wanted a guarantee that whatever happens, you're on our side. You won't let Huang use this as a weapon."

"How do we know that you won't use it as a weapon?"

"I understand that you have no reason to trust me. I was here during the war, working for the government, but John Caring trusted me and I know that you know John Caring is not a traitor. I want what's best for this country, and I would never use the brutal techniques

Huang has to get there."

Isabelle and Michael nodded.

"All right, we'll consider it, and we won't go to Huang in the meantime."

"Thank you."

———

BALLOT	
Attorney General	Isaac Rosenthal
Minister of Defense and Homeland Security	David Cullen
Minister of Education	Katherine Lehmberg
Minister of Agriculture and Commerce	Elizabeth Ellis
Minister of Energy and the Interior	Gemma Grant
Minister of Health, Housing, and Human Services	Zoe Cheon

Ben voted as soon as the polls opened at 6:00 am for everyone Rosenthal had instructed. Once the cabinet members were elected, they would organize a coup and have Huang removed from power.

This could take a few weeks or a few months, they weren't sure.

John Caring's trial date had been set for one month after the election, Tuesday, July 26, and Emily's hearing was the following day.

They had secured guarantees from Cullen, Cheon, Grant, and Ellis that they would support Rosenthal's coup of Huang; Lehmberg was the holdout. She was an old military buddy of Huang's and didn't want to commit to the coup if Huang's safety couldn't be guaranteed. These weren't the only candidates though. There were several military generals up for each post. Most were ludicrously unqualified, but they were included on the ballot at Huang's insistence. There had been propaganda campaigns in the media promoting them, but still their chances were slim. Huang's position as General was not up for this election.

Ben spent the day at the Rosenthal's office with the rest of the campaign staff. Huang was out of the country in Canada, trying to build trust and create trade agreements.

"The polling had me in the lead, but you never know which way the voters will turn. I was part of the old administration; they may hold that against me."

"I understand that, sir, but we did some excellent campaigning. The people know you're on their side."

As the day went on, it became clear that Rosenthal would win Attorney General. He had both Huang's backing and the public's. The other races were much closer. Lehmberg was guaranteed early on, having both military and general public support. She had been a member of the old administration as well.

In the end, everyone on Ben's ballot was elected except Grant. The position of Minister of Energy and the Interior went to one of Huang's closest advisors, Colonel Mocerino. Given that the Ultimate Ending Project was funded through that department, this was expected.

At the end of the night there was a champagne toast at the old Detroit City Hall, now the Capital Building, and Rosenthal gave a brief speech. All of the elected cabinet members were there and several of the losing candidates. Catherine Caring was there as well. As the victory celebration wound down, Catherine pulled Rosenthal aside.

"So what does this mean? Now that you're officially Attorney General, will you be able to get Emily out of prison? What about John?"

"Catherine, please, not here."

"If not now, when? You haven't returned my calls in over a week!"

Rosenthal wouldn't face her. He tilted his head toward her and chuckled as if she was saying something funny, offering congratulations. He was nodding and thanking people as they passed. Finally, there was a break and he turned his head and looked directly at her. He held on to her shoulder with his hand, seeming to comfort her.

"When we meet as a group, all the newly elected officials, in two weeks, I will handle it. Until then, do not bring this up again." He released her shoulder but she didn't move.

"Very well, but Isaac, when will I see you again?"

He looked directly above her head and answered, "I told you I would be busy with the campaign. Now that it's over, I can see you tomorrow night. I'll meet you at 9 o'clock."

She smiled, like a teenaged school girl with a crush on her teacher. "Thank you."

———

Catherine and Rosenthal met in their usual spot, a private park adjacent to his apartment building. The park was only open to those who lived in the building, and no children went to the park after dark. Rosenthal would block the security cameras with a device he had confiscated during the war, and they would talk and kiss for an hour or two. Sometimes, if he knew they wouldn't be seen, Rosenthal would invite Catherine up and they would sleep together. Then Rosenthal would drive Catherine home before curfew. She never slept over because she didn't want to alarm Wallace.

He was waiting for her on a bench, at the entrance to the park. She smiled slyly as she walked up to him, and touched his arm as she sat down next to him. She reached for his hand to hold it and he pulled away.

"What's wrong?" she asked.

"Catherine, the things that are about to happen, in the next few weeks. If we can accomplish what we've set out to, many things are going to change... for the country, and between us."

"What do you mean?"

"If everything goes according to plan, we can't see each other anymore, not like this. I will have greater responsibilities than I have now, or did have before. And if I can get Emily and John released from prison, then you will have to go back to your family life. We can't have any more... disruptions."

"But can't we just go on like before? Before the war we were together and nothing..."

Rosenthal held up his hand to stop her from continuing. "No, things will be different now. These decisions, and their ramifications, its life and death; what I'm trying to do here, for our country, is too important. I can't have any scandals or distractions. I'm sorry."

"So you're saying it will be over, in just two weeks?"

"I'm saying it's over now."

Catherine started to cry.

"I'm sorry. Let me know when you're ready to go and I'll drive you."

"No, I can leave on my own."

"Catherine, you can't mention this to anyone, do you understand? If you do, I can't guarantee Emily's safety."

At this Catherine froze, her face turned to stone. "I would never endanger my family. I've never told anyone about us, other than Ben, as you know, and I won't tell anyone now."

Rosenthal started to stand, but Catherine put her hand on his shoulder.

"No, I can walk. Thank you."

And with that, their relationship, as they knew it, was over.

———

July 11, 2061

Ben was editing the last few documents for the packets to be given to the new cabinet members at their first meeting. The meeting was at 9:00 am, in thirty minutes. Ben had been in the office since 7:00

am. There had been several last minute changes General Huang had wanted to make to two documents in the packet regarding a trade agreement with Mexico. He wanted all the cabinet members to have both hard and electronic copies of the documents; little did he know that at 9:05 am, officers would be coming in to the cabinet meeting to arrest him and Colonel Mocerino.

It had all been arranged by Rosenthal, with Lehmberg's help, shortly after the election. It turned out very few people truly wanted Huang in power; they just wanted the war to end. All of his strict regulations had been too much. He had gone too far with his brutality and mistrust of the people; even those in his inner circle were ready to turn over the reins to Rosenthal, with the understanding that they would not be arrested once he had taken control.

Rosenthal was standing in the cabinet room next to Ben.

"Everything ready?"

"Almost."

"And Stevenson will be here?"

"Yes, he said he will be here at 10:00 am, as you requested."

"Good, good," Rosenthal nodded. "You know, Ben, I couldn't have done this without you. You've done a great thing for your country, and once we have this project Stevenson is working on under control, you'll be a hero. You should be very proud."

"I am, thank you, sir." Ben finished the packets, putting one in front of each of the seven chairs, one for each cabinet member and one for the secretary taking the minutes. He handed a medium-sized device to Rosenthal. "Here you are, sir, you can project onto the back screen with this device."

Rosenthal smiled, "Thank you, Ben, you go and wait in my office. Secure the doors and be ready to answer any questions. I'll see you when this is all over."

Ben nodded and left the cabinet room.

Gradually, each cabinet member arrived and by 9:00 am everyone was there but Huang. Had he found out about the coup? By 9:02 am, Cullen was visibly nervous. He kept tapping his left index finger on the table. Rosenthal shot him a look just as Huang strode in.

"Hello, good morning all." He walked over to Rosenthal confidently. "Mr. Rosenthal, my new official Attorney General." The men shook hands and Huang walked back to the head of the table.

"Now ladies, and gentlemen, I am pleased that you are all here. The New Republic epitomizes the values we fought for during the revolution. I have recently completed several trade agreements with Russia, Canada, and Mexico, which Mr. Rosenthal will be detailing in the presentation, and which you have in the packets in front of you. I look forward to working with each of you to secure our newly found freedom, and future prosperity." He turned his gaze to Rosenthal. "Mr. Rosenthal, please begin."

Rosenthal nodded, and pushed a button on the side of his device. This was the signal for the guards to enter and arrest Huang and Mocerino. On cue the doors burst open. Four guards entered, guns raised.

Huang leapt up from his chair. "What is the meaning of this?"

Mocerino reached into his waist band to pull out his gun, but Rosenthal saw him and shook his head saying, "Don't even think about it, Colonel."

Two of the guards went to Mocerino, and two to Huang. One held his gun up, while the other handcuffed them.

Huang was screaming at Rosenthal, "You're a traitor, Isaac, a traitor! You wouldn't even be in this position if it weren't for me!"

"You're not going to get away with this, any of you," Mocerino muttered, glaring at Lehmberg.

Rosenthal nodded at the guards who took both men away, and then moved to the head of the table and sat down.

"All right, as the acting President of the New Republic, I now call this meeting of the cabinet into session."

The mood in the room had lifted considerably. There was a round of applause and several cheers. Rosenthal smiled widely. "Yes, this is a victory for us all. Now, if you would please open your packets and look at the screen up here, we can get started. We have a country to run."

Rosenthal conducted the meeting as if nothing had happened. Meanwhile, Ben and the campaign team were barricaded in Rosenthal's office, fielding questions from the media on their devices.

As the meeting came to a close, Rosenthal said, "As you know, I've nominated Dr. Michael Stevenson for the post of Minister of Energy and the Interior. He should be arriving shortly, in fact," he glanced at his device and saw the time, 11:15 am. "He should be waiting outside. One moment, please, excuse me."

Rosenthal left the cabinet room. There were two guards standing out front. They both saluted him. "Where is Dr. Stevenson?"

"He is in the waiting room, sir, across the hall." He walked across the hall and opened the door to the waiting room, but it was empty. He looked back at the guards. "No, he's not."

Both guards ran to the doorway and their faces fell.

"You, stay here," he said, pointing to the male guard, "and you, come with me." He walked down the hallway to his office, and plugged in the code to unlock the door. It wasn't working. He knocked several times and Ben opened the door.

"Hello, sir, is something wrong?"

"Why wouldn't the code work?"

"I changed it, sir, a security measure, in case something went wrong."

"Good thinking, but you should have told me. Dr. Stevenson isn't in the waiting area, he's gone."

"What do you mean? He arrived at around 9:45 and one of the guards took him to the waiting area. He's not in there?"

"No, no one's there."

"What?" Ben quickly left Rosenthal's office and ran to the waiting room with Rosenthal and the female guard close behind him. "But he was just here, I watched him go in and sit down. There was sup-posed to be a guard outside the whole time!"

Just then Rosenthal received a message on his device from a blocked address: *I have left the country with the project. My wife is with me. We cannot risk it falling into the wrong hands. - Dr. Michael Stevenson.*

"Damn it!" Rosenthal exclaimed, passing his device to Ben who read the message. He turned to the guard with him. "Go have Annabelle and Christopher Stevenson detained. Have them brought to the prison for questioning."

Ben inhaled sharply. Rosenthal turned to him, "Do you have a problem with that Hughes?"

"No, sir, I understand."

"Good. We need that project contained, and they may know something. Any information they can provide could be essential to its retrieval."

Over the next two weeks there was a manhunt for Michael and Isabelle Stevenson, but no leads. Annabelle and Christopher were questioned, and then held in prison for two weeks. Andy stopped speaking to Ben because of his involvement with Rosenthal and his culpability in Annabelle's imprisonment. The transition after Huang's removal had been smooth. Rosenthal had made sure of that before the coup. Huang and Mocerino were in prison, and would be tried for war crimes, among other offenses, before the International Criminal Court in a few months.

Ben felt torn between his loyalty to Rosenthal and his disapproval of the treatment of Annabelle and Christopher. He had made it to where he wanted to be though. Huang had been ousted and he was in a position of power in the new administration, but his friends were in prison. He was all alone, and Rosenthal's obsession with "the project" was beginning to worry him. Was this right? He had been promoted to Chief of Staff in Rosenthal's administration and so he worked long hours to block out the questions that plagued him.

Before he knew it, it was the weekend before John Caring's trial, and Rosenthal had decided he would prosecute John Caring to the fullest extent of the law.

The Trial of John Caring

Emily Caring had lost track of time. She knew it had been months since she had been arrested, but time was no longer linear. It seemed abstract since her days had become so monotonous. The female guard who had dried her off after the shower incident had been kind to her. She had brought her a few books, and sometimes, when she was on duty, would allow her to stay outside longer than the allotted thirty minutes. She couldn't protect her from the male guards though, who would reach out and fondle her as she walked by. She hadn't been outright assaulted again, but she never knew if that was coming. Kyle had visited her once, but she had refused to see him.

One day, the kind female guard came to her isolation cell. She didn't have any books with her.

"Ms. Caring, you have a visitor."

Emily stood up. She hadn't had a visitor since Kyle.   "Who? Who is it? Is it my mother?"

"No, it's your father's attorney, Mr. Roberts."

"Is he my attorney now, too?"

"I can't say for sure, but I would assume so."

"So they've set a date for my hearing?"

"I don't know. You'll have to ask Mr. Roberts."

She didn't want to get her hopes up, but Emily smiled anyway. "Okay, I'm ready. Let's go."

Emily walked down the long hallway to the meeting room with her head held high. The guard at the meeting room door didn't grope her, which was unusual. He pushed a button and the door slid open. It was the same meeting room where she had met with her father months before. Mr. Roberts was seated when Emily entered. He stood up and extended his hand. She shook it.

"Good to see you, Ms. Caring, please have a seat."

She sat across from him. "What's this all about? Are you my lawyer? Have they set a date for my hearing?"

"Yes, I am, but not for long. The state has dropped its charges against you. You're going to be freed this afternoon."

Emily leapt out of her chair, "Really? Today? Why?"

"The Attorney General, Isaac Rosenthal, has dropped the charges."

"Rosenthal? Does he have the power to do that?"

"Oh, so you haven't heard. I would have assumed... well, it doesn't matter. There was a coup after the election. It was nonviolent. Huang was removed from power and he's in prison, here actually. I thought someone would have told you; one of the guards, at least."

Emily shook her head in disbelief. "So who is the President?"

"There is an acting President, Ms. Carol Harper. She was voted in by the cabinet."

"So everything's changed now."

"Well, no. Everything is pretty much the same. There's been no revolution, no uprising against Huang's removal. Attorney General Rosenthal has more power now, and he has pardoned you, on one condition."

"Yes?"

"You have to testify in your father's trial."

"What? Why? I don't know anything about his life at work when he was Attorney General, only at home, as my Dad."

"Well, I think the argument is that when you met with him here he must have told you something that would prove his corruption."

"Well he didn't. He told me to trust Rosenthal because he wanted to overthrow Huang."

"He didn't talk about the census?"

"What? No. What about the census?"

"I've said too much."

"Mr. Roberts, please, what is my father being accused of?"

"I can't get into that. Not here, not now. And if Rosenthal talks to you, do not mention the census. It could jeopardize your father's case. Either way, you need to decide this in the next few minutes. I have all the paperwork securing your release here in my device. I just need you to sign saying that you will testify and I'll have you out of here by the end of the day."

Emily sat there, frozen. What could she do? Rosenthal had been a friend of their family so he must have some positive motive. She wouldn't lie on the stand; she would tell the truth. She would sign the document now, secure her release, and tell the truth on the witness stand.

She nodded, "I'll do it, where do I sign?"

Mr. Roberts pulled out his device, scrolled through several documents, and then passed the device to Emily.

"I advise you to please read this carefully before signing."

FEDERAL COURT
OF THE NEW REPUBLIC

NEW REPUBLIC v. John R. Caring	Case No. 13159

SUBPOENA TO TESTIFY AT A HEARING OR TRIAL IN A CRIMINAL CASE

To: **Emily Caring**

Your release from the Federal Prison of the New Republic is secured with your signature of this document. All criminal charges brought against you by the state have been dropped. If you fail to appear in court and testify at the date and time below, this contract is null and void.

Place of Appearance: Federal Courthouse of Honor and Liberty
Courtroom No.: 1
Date and Time: 7/27/2061 at 9:00 AM

_____
Signature

_____
Date

Emily read the document closely, and then signed it with the stylus.

"Very good, thank you, Ms. Caring. Your father's trial starts tomorrow, but you aren't expected in court until Wednesday. I will be back at the end of the day to pick you up."

––––––––

July 25, 2061

"Ben, I need you finish that summary before noon so I can review it."

"Yes, sir."

"It's not a crucial part of the case, but it's important."

"Yes, sir. I'm almost finished. I'll have it to you within an hour."

"Good."

Rosenthal was standing in the doorway of Ben's office. They had been doing the final preparations for John Caring's trial all weekend. Rosenthal was prosecuting the case himself. He could have passed it on to one of the other lawyers on his team, but this was a big case and he wanted to show his strength and handle it personally. After the coup, everyone was looking to see what he would do next. He didn't want to appear soft on those from the old Michigan administration. It was their actions the people had revolted against.

"Do you need anything else, sir?"

Rosenthal shook his head. "No, thank you, Ben."

"You're welcome."

"What exactly do they want you to say?" Catherine asked Emily.

They were sitting on Emily's bed. Emily had gotten home late last night. After she signed the document, securing her testimony and her release, she had been taken back to her isolation cell. No one had spoken to her or even looked at her. About an hour later, Isaac Rosenthal himself had come to speak with her—not in the meeting room, in her cell. She recalled the conversation for her mother.

"Hello, Ms. Caring."

"Hello Mr. Rosenthal... you've known me most of my life, you can call me Emily, like you used to."

"Yes, well, under these circumstances I think it's best to be formal, but yes, hello, Emily."

Emily smiled lightly.

"Do you understand what you signed? What you're being asked to do?"

Emily nodded, "Testify against my father."

"Yes, well it's not so much testify *against* as to tell the truth."

Emily paused, taking in his response, "I understand."

"We are in a very sensitive time in this country. The revolution is over, but our borders are in jeopardy. We need to have a united front against the administration that got us into this, that pushed people to the breaking point, made them revolt. People need to know that inequality, unstable governance and revolutions are behind them. We are moving forward as one, united New Republic. Do you understand that?"

"Yes."

Rosenthal nodded. "Thank you." He started to walk away and then paused. "When you get home this evening, be sure to give my regards to Wallace, and to your mother."

Catherine listened intently as Emily finished, "So what are you going to do?"

"I'm going to tell the truth."

"Which is?"

"Whatever he asks me I'll answer truthfully. I never saw Dad do anything remotely illegal."

"He may try to turn things around though. Make you say things you don't mean. Rosenthal can be very persuasive."

"Don't worry, Mom," Emily said, resting her hand on Catherine's shoulder, "I can handle it."

———

July 26, 2061

"All rise, hear ye, hear ye, this court is now in session. The Honorable Judge Olivia Sen presiding."

Judge Sen was young for someone in her position, in her mid-thirties. She had long, dark auburn hair and fair skin. Her father was

Japanese and her mother was Syrian. Her father, Judge Albert Sen, had been highly respected before the revolution. Her family was not detained during the war, but her father had chosen to retire. She had taken his seat.

Judge Sen looked out into the packed courtroom. "Please be seated."

The crowd took their seats. Emily, Catherine, and Wallace were seated two rows behind the defense's table where Mr. Roberts and John Caring were seated; Ben was at the prosecution's table with Rosenthal. Annabelle, Christopher, and Andy were in the back, standing.

"The case is the New Republic vs. John R. Caring. The charges are corruption, and murder in the first degree. How does the defendant plea?"

Mr. Roberts rose and addressed the judge, "Not guilty."

"Let the record show that the defendant has entered a plea of not guilty," replied Judge Sen. She then turned her attention to Rosenthal. "The state may begin."

Rosenthal rose and walked out from behind the table. He was wearing a navy blue, double breasted suit with very thin, white pinstripes. He strode over toward the jury, who were seated in a spacious jury box, and angled his body so he was addressing both the jury and the courtroom.

"We are here today because someone who was in a position of power abused it, and we, the people, suffered because of his actions. Through certified documentation and eye witness accounts, I will show you just how egregious his actions were. The defendant, John Caring, spearheaded efforts to subjugate the people of the former state of Michigan, and when challenged, would arrange for the elimination of those people either through expulsion from the state, or murder. Yes, that's right. He would have people killed who disagreed with him or with former Michigan Governor Adams. In the New Republic, these vile acts will not be tolerated, and with your help, ladies and gentlemen of the jury, he will be brought to justice. Thank you."

Rosenthal moved back to his seat next to Ben and sat down.

Emily's eyes widened. Her father was being charged with murder. It wasn't possible. He wasn't capable of murder. He taught her how to ride of bike, and read stories to her and her brothers before bed. He wasn't a murderer. And he worked to help the people of Michigan, not harm them. This was insane.

Mr. Roberts stood and moved to where Rosenthal had stood during his opening remarks, first addressing Judge Sen. "Good morning, your Honor, good morning ladies and gentlemen of the jury," he paused and looked out into the courtroom. "John Caring is a civil servant who served the people of Michigan, many of whom are in this courtroom, for over twenty years. He fought for stringent emissions standards so we could breathe clean air, he secured farming subsidies from the federal government so we could put food on our tables, he was known as a kind man by those who knew him, and a generous man by reputation alone. John Caring was part of an administration who committed acts that hurt the people of Michigan, but he did not initiate them. He tried, and often succeeded, in preventing many evils the previous administration sought to commit.

But we all know that every crusade must have a scape goat, and since Governor Adams is not here to admit to his crimes all we have is John Caring, a good man who lived by his principles, to take the blame for these alleged acts."

Mr. Roberts shook his head, "The real crime, ladies and gentlemen, would be to allow this man, who has already spent over four years in prison, to be convicted of crimes he did not commit. He is a champion of the people, who protected your rights and fought for your quality of life. Remember that, as you hear the lies the prosecution will tell you. John Caring helped you live a better life, now you can help him by giving him his life back. Thank you."

Catherine exhaled slowly. She had been holding her breath through most of the opening statements. She had spousal immunity and therefore had not been called testify. She was glad, because she did not know what she would say, or how she could explain herself and what she knew.

"The prosecution may call its first witness."

"The state calls Andrew Lemmings to the stand."

An off-duty police officer walked up to the stand. He was of average height and build. The kind of nondescript Caucasian male used in a line up at a police station when a witness is asked to identify a suspect behind reflective glass. He placed his right hand on the bible and repeated after the bailiff, "To tell the truth, the whole truth, and nothing but the truth. So help me God." Then he sat down and Rosenthal began.

"Mr. Lemmings, what was your occupation before the revolution?"

"I was a Detroit Police Officer."

"Yes and what was your record? Did you have any complaints filed against you?"

"I had a clean record. No complaints."

"You're quite modest, Mr. Lemmings. You not only had a clean record, you were given an award. Isn't that right?"

"Yes, sir."

"You don't seem very proud of that."

"I was just doing my job."

Rosenthal nodded. "Yes, of course. Now, in doing your job, were you ever asked to do anything that was morally wrong?"

Mr. Roberts stood up. "Objection, we are in a court of law, not morality."

"Sustained."

"Let me rephrase. Were you ever asked to do anything *you felt* was morally wrong?"

"Yes, sir."

"Can you explain that situation to the court?"

"Yes. Detroit was losing state and federal funding because the population was too low. I was asked to head up the team of police officers who were rounding up homeless people in the suburbs and dropping them off in the ghetto, within city limits. We were told to count them, report that number to the Census Bureau, then after the census was over and the city got its money, we were supposed to move them back."

"And you completed this task?"

"Yes, sir, I did, twice."

"And what happened if one of these people resisted? What if they didn't want to come with you?"

"Well, if they didn't want to come with us into the city, before the census, we were told to sedate them and bring them anyway. Then after, when we were taking them back outside the city, if they resisted too much we were told to... dispose of them."

"Dispose of them?"

"Yes, dispose of them. Get rid of them. Kill them if we had to. Since they were homeless, I guess the city figured no one would come looking for them."

There was a gasp from the crowd in the court room.

"And who ordered you to dispose of them?"

"Attorney General John Caring."

"Not Governor Adams?"

"No, I'm sure he knew about it, but the order itself was signed by John Caring."

"And did you ever object to these policies? Say anything to your superiors?"

"No, sir, not at first. I decided I would just ignore the disposal order, just sedate them on the way in and on the way out."

"And this worked every time?"

Mr. Lemmings shook his head. "No, unfortunately, one of the rookies, well one time this guy got really rough with him and he shot him. And the man died."

"Did you report this to Mr. Caring?"

"Yes, and I told him that I thought this policy was terrible. These were people, human beings, not cattle to be moved around."

"And what did Mr. Caring say?"

"He told me that society must evolve, and he gave me a raise and an award for service to Detroit."

"I see. And how long did these policies continue?"

"Until 2056, when Mr. Caring was arrested; it was going on until the revolution."

"And do you think this policy of resettling people and murder would have continued if Mr. Caring had remained Attorney General?"

"Yes, sir."

"Thank you, Mr. Lemmings."

Judge Sen raised her eyebrows. "Your witness, Mr. Roberts."

Mr. Roberts stood up slowly with his hands in his pockets. He had on a dark brown suit.

"Mr. Lemmings, you say that the order was signed by John Caring."

"Yes, sir."

"You saw this order?"

"Yes, sir. It was downloaded to our devices."

Mr. Roberts nodded. "Do you think Mr. Caring could just sign an order without Governor Adams' approval?"

Mr. Lemmings paused for a moment. "I'm not sure."

"Well legally, an order of that magnitude would have to have the approval of the Governor before being signed into law."

"Oh no it wasn't a law, it was just an order."

"I see. So it wasn't a law, just an order from the Attorney General to relocate homeless people and kill them if they resisted?"

"Yes."

"There is no record of this order in the state files from that time period."

"Well no, it was wiped from our devices after the census."

"I see. So there is no physical evidence that this order was given, and you, yourself, admit that it would probably have to come from Governor Adams if it did."

"No, I just said I wasn't sure."

"You're not sure, so you have some doubts?"

"Look, I know what I read and what I was ordered to do. That happened."

"And the meeting with John Caring, you recorded this?"

"No."

"Why not?"

"I didn't think it was necessary."

"You didn't think recording a conversation where a public official might admit to ordering murder was necessary?"

"It was self-defense, not murder. That rookie just got scared and didn't know any better."

"So it wasn't murder?"

"No, but the order said we could kill them so it could have been."

"So someone was killed and you're saying that wasn't murder?"

"Look, I know what you're doing. We were ordered by John Caring to kill innocent people if they resisted us moving them, period. That's what happened!"

Mr. Roberts nodded. "And when you talked to Mr. Caring, what exactly did he say?"

"Well he thanked me, you know for me coming in and speaking with him. Then he said that societies evolve over time and my service was invaluable."

"That was it?"

"No, then I asked him if anything would change."

"And what was his answer?"

"That he would look into it, he said that societies evolve and change over time and that he appreciated my coming to him directly. Then the next day I got a raise, and the week after that I got an award."

"And did the order ever change?"

"Well no, because the revolution happened."

"So an order that John Caring allegedly signed, whether he created it or not is debatable, but let's just say he did sign it. When you brought your concerns to his attention he thanked you, and then gave you a raise and an award. Is that correct?"

"Yes."

"So it sounds like," and at this Mr. Roberts turned to face the jury, "It sounds like Mr. Caring valued this issue being brought to his attention so much that he rewarded you, Mr. Lemmings, and if he hadn't been arrested by General Huang's forces, Mr. Caring would have stopped this practice, and brought whoever gave that order to justice; which was, in fact, his job as Attorney General. He was doing his job. He heard your complaint and was going to act on it."

"If he gave the damn order, then why would he change it? He was just saying that to get me out of his office!"

"*If* he gave the order," Mr. Roberts nodded. "Thank you Mr. Lemmings, you may step down."

Catherine was gripping Emily's hand and breathing heavily. Emily looked at her mother and a thought entered her mind, *what does she know?*

Judge Sen's voice jolted her back, "The prosecution may call its next witness."

The next two witnesses were also former Detroit police officers who had done her father's alleged bidding. If they were to be believed, John Caring had ordered the murder of anyone who resisted his policies, which included the demolition of government housing to build lucrative tourism projects. It was just what the soldier had told Emily in Mason, when she encountered him on her way to the refugee camp. That was all hearsay though, there was no concrete proof. It was their word against her father's. The prosecution had three more witnesses: her father's former secretary, Mrs. Egan, Emily, and finally Roselyn, a prostitute, her father had allegedly hired for Governor Adams and himself.

"This concludes today's proceedings. The prosecution will call its remaining three witnesses tomorrow, Mrs. Janice Egan, Ms. Emily Caring, and Ms. Roselyn Childs." Judge Sen banged her gavel, and everyone rose as she left the courtroom.

———

That night, Emily lay in bed thinking about her testimony. Rosenthal hadn't prepped her at all. She thought he wanted to catch her off guard. If she didn't say what he wanted her to, would he send her back to prison? It was scary but she was brave. She had come this far. She wouldn't be the reason her father remained in prison.

———

July 27, 2061

"All rise. This court is now in session, the honorable Judge Olivia Sen presiding."

Emily rose, but was shaking. She was standing between her mother and Wallace.

Judge Sen sat down and banged her gavel. "Be seated. The prosecution may call its first witness."

Rosenthal stood. "The prosecution calls Mrs. Janice Egan."

An elderly woman approached the witness stand. Her graying hair was pulled up into a high bun, and she wore a navy blue pant suit. After being sworn in, she sat down slowly.

"Good morning, Mrs. Egan, thank you for coming here today."

Mrs. Egan sat with her arms folded across her chest. "You're welcome."

"How long were you Mr. Caring's secretary?"

"Fifteen years."

"That's a long time."

"Yes."

"What kind of work did you do for him?"

"Secretarial work."

"Yes, but that could be anything. Did you type up reports? File paperwork?"

"Yes, I filed all paperwork."

"So, if Mr. Caring wrote anything, a memo, an order perhaps, you would have filed it?"

"Yes."

"There have been many accusations against Mr. Caring, including that he sent out signed orders to the devices of people in government service. Would you have filed those as well?"

"If he sent them out personally, no. If it was professional, then yes."

"Did you ever file an order regarding the census?"

"I filed several orders regarding the census. It's a complicated procedure."

"Yes, of course. Did you ever file an order regarding the relocation of homeless people for the census?"

"Yes."

Rosenthal nodded. "And do you remember what it said?"

"I don't remember the exact words, but it was about housing homeless people from the suburbs in the city; giving them housing, none of this dropping them off on the streets nonsense."

"There's no record of any order regarding relocating homeless people."

"Well maybe when the revolutionaries came in they destroyed everything. How should I know?"

"So you didn't delete that file?"

"I was subpoenaed, Mr. Rosenthal, and I'm here. Mr. Caring is a good man."

Judge Sen addressed the witness, "Answer the question, Mrs. Egan, you're under oath."

"Sometimes we would delete files that didn't matter anymore. Once the census was taken, we didn't need all the paperwork that led up to it."

"Did you or did you not delete the file with the order about relocating homeless people for the census?"

"I deleted many files regarding the census, and that could have, perhaps, been one of them. I don't remember."

"No further questions."

"Your witness, Mr. Roberts."

Mr. Roberts rose but did not move from behind the table, "Mrs. Egan, in the fifteen years you worked for Mr. Caring, did you ever see him break the law?"

"No, sir, I did not."

"Act maliciously to any person in any way?"

"No, sir, I did not."

"No further questions."

"You may step down, Mrs. Egan."

Rosenthal glanced back into the crowd at Emily, and then turned to address Judge Sen. "The prosecution calls Ms. Emily Caring to the stand."

Catherine and Wallace stood up with Emily and guided her to the aisle. She was shaking as she stood, but by the time she made it to the aisle she was composed. There were murmurs and whispers in the crowd. Emily held her head high as she approached the witness stand. When she reached the bailiff, she was ready. She placed her right hand on the bible, "I solemnly swear to tell the truth, the whole truth, and nothing but the truth. So help me God." She sat down and looked at her father first and then Rosenthal. She avoided Ben's gaze, it would only rattle her confidence. John Caring looked at her lovingly and gave her a solid nod.

Rosenthal stood up, and began. "Hello, Ms. Caring, how are you today?"

"I'm well, thank you."

"Glad to hear it. I understand this must be difficult for you, and the state appreciates your testimony. I will advise the court that I have known this witness a long time, since she was a child, and I would not have asked her to come here today if it wasn't of the utmost importance. Now, Ms. Caring, this may seem like an odd question, but how long have you known the defendant?"

"My entire life, over twenty-six years."

"So when he was working for the state of Michigan, you knew him very well?"

"Yes, but not in his government role, I knew him as my father."

"Yes, of course. Did you consider him a role model?"

"Yes."

"A mentor?"

"Yes, aside from being my father he's a very well-educated and accomplished person."

"Very true, he is that. So if you had a problem, say with your friends or in school, you would ask him for his advice?"

Emily tried to think where he could be going with this. She was scanning her memory for any incident that Rosenthal might have been privy to.

"Yes, depending on the subject. I would ask him, my mother, maybe one of my teachers. He wasn't the only person I asked for help."

"Well of course not, that's perfectly understandable. There was one topic that bothered you though where you did ask his opinion, and that was in the area of volunteer work in the Detroit community. Is that correct?"

"I may have asked him, I don't recall."

"Just to be clear for the jury, in the previous school system to qualify for the United States National Honors Society you had to maintain a 3.5 grade point average and complete thirty hours of community service. Were you a member of the National Honors Society in high school, Ms. Caring?"

"Yes."

"And where did you complete your community service?"

"At an animal shelter."

Rosenthal nodded, "At an animal shelter. Was that your first choice?"

"I don't recall." Emily's mind was racing, she had done that one day at the soup kitchen, it had disturbed her and her father had advised her not to go again. Then she had picked the animal shelter. How could Rosenthal know that? Had her father mentioned it to him when they worked together?

"Let me present this communication between Mr. Caring and myself dated September 12, 2051. Ms. Caring was sixteen years old, a junior in high school. She had volunteered at a soup kitchen and found the conditions to be terrible. She then asked her father for his advice, and he relayed that story to me via this written communication from that time. Ms. Caring, please read this for the court."

Rosenthal passed her his device, and Emily read aloud.

> "She was so upset, Isaac, but I explained to her that it wasn't the job of the government to take care of homeless people in the city. That's why private organizations exist, to help them. We just move them around to help with the population numbers."
>
> "Did you tell her that?"
>
> "Well not in those words, of course. I told her she should try the animal shelter. They have a great set up over there. It will be safe."

Emily was holding back tears. She shoved the device back into Rosenthal's hand.

"So, ladies and gentlemen, as you can see, Mr. Caring did not think it was his responsibility to take care of the people of Michigan. They were merely numbers to him, disposable numbers. And even when his own daughter tried to help them, he discouraged her."

Rosenthal nodded at Emily, without making eye contact. "Thank you, Ms. Caring."

"Your witness, Mr. Roberts."

"Ms. Caring, thank you for your time today. I will only ask you two questions."

Emily nodded. "Thank you, Mr. Roberts."

"Why are you testifying today?"

"Because I was subpoenaed."

"And what were the conditions under which you were subpoenaed?"

"If I testified against my father, Mr. Rosenthal would release me from prison, where I have been illegally detained without a hearing for the last several months."

There were murmurs in the crowd.

"Thank you Ms. Caring, you may step down."

Judge Sen banged her gavel. "Order in the court. This court will take a one hour recess, and then continue with the state's final witness."

Emily couldn't look at her father, so she stared at the floor as she made her way back to her mother and Wallace. They both gave her a hug and they all sat down. A security guard blocked the path of anyone trying to approach them.

Catherine turned to Emily, "I'm very proud of you. You were very brave up there, and don't worry about Rosenthal. He won't put you back in prison, I promise."

"How do you know?"

"I've know that man a long time. He wouldn't harm my children."

Emily shook her head; it wasn't worth arguing with her mother. Not now.

"Are you going to stay and hear the next witness?" Wallace asked them.

"No, I can't listen to a prostitute tell lies about your father," Catherine replied.

Emily looked at Wallace, "I'll stay, if you will."

Wallace nodded. "I want to stay. After living in the dark for so many years, I want to hear everything anyone is saying."

Emily smiled at Wallace and reached out to touch his hand. Then there was a loud explosion. It rocked the whole building and filled it with smoke. Emily, Catherine and Wallace were thrown to the ground.

A voice, seemingly coming from the ceiling, boomed all around them. "This is General Winston Huang, the true leader of the New Republic. John Caring is a criminal. Isaac Rosenthal is a criminal. They will be brought to justice. I have in my possession eight bombs more powerful than anything used by man before. The scientists who created them secured my escape from prison. All must surrender or I will detonate one bomb every twenty-four hours, at an undisclosed location, anywhere in the world, until they do. This is my only warning."

Another explosion followed, with more smoke. Emily started crawling toward the aisle. She reached her hand out to feel her surroundings and someone grabbed her wrist. She shook her arm free and looked up, it was her father.

"Is your mother okay? Where is Wallace? We have to get out of here, now."

Catherine's voice answered weakly behind them, "We're here, John. We're okay."

Emily could barely see in front of her face, but the four of them crawled toward the door. She heard moaning near the front of the courtroom and screams from the gallery, but she blocked out all noise that wasn't her father's voice, guiding her out of the building.

Winston's Story

Winston Lewis Huang was born in a small hospital outside of Chicago on January 1, 2005. His parents were only teenagers when he was born, but they loved him very much and cared for him the best way they knew how. That was when he was their only child. Over the next seven years, they had three more children. His mother sunk slowly into alcoholism, trying to escape from her overwhelming responsibilities, and his father spent an increasing amount of time away from their home until one day, he never came back.

By the time Winston was eight years old, he was caring for his younger siblings more than his mother. She had fallen into a deep depression and only on rare occasions would she leave the house. Usually, she confined herself to a chair in the living room where she watched television and was either extremely drunk or asleep. Winston could never tell. Her black hair was matted to her head, and she smelled overly sweet, like fruit beginning to rot. When he reached up to kiss her cheek the smell made him nauseous. He did it anyway though, because he knew she liked it. "Mommy loves you so much," she would say, the words often slurring together.

His mother had a part time job doing data entry at home. After his father left, she managed to put in a few hours every day and still make some money for the first month. After that, she said she didn't have the energy. Then he came home from school one day and the baby was crying, his dirty diaper sagging so low it nearly touched the ground.

"Did you feed him today?" Winston asked his mother, who did not answer other than soft snoring and the occasional gurgle. The other two children, ages three and four, had managed to eat through any candy in the house and were napping on Winston's bed. It was then that he missed three days of school to take care of his siblings. His concerned teacher, unable to reach his parents, called child services, who intervened.

The day the social worker came, he was just getting up. His routine over the last three days had been to go into the living room and check on his mother, then get cereal out for his siblings, a bottle of milk for the baby, and then wake them up and feed them. Then they would all gather around the television in his room and watch several programs until the baby cried. Then he would change his diaper and they would all go to the park and play until it was time for lunch. He would check on his mother again while his younger siblings ate, and offer her some food which she declined. Then all the children would nap while Winston looked through the cupboards to find something for dinner.

When the social worker arrived, Winston was standing in the living room. There was almost no food left in the house and he was going to try to wake his mother up and ask for money when there was a knock at the door. His first thought was that it must be his father, finally coming home to help them. He ran to the door, grasped the doorknob, and pulled it open with all his might.

A tall, slender, woman with tan skin and a wide smile knelt down so she was eye level with him.

"You must be Winston," she said.

He pulled back. "Who are you?"

"I'm Selena Lieberman. Your teacher, Mrs. Woods, called me. I'm here to check on you. Are your Mom or Dad at home?"

"My Mom is home, but she's sleeping and my Dad is," he paused, "at work I think."

"Okay well, I really need to talk to your Mom, so maybe you could wake her up or I could come in and talk to her with you?"

Winston nodded, moving aside to let the woman inside. He was wary of strangers, but he was also aware that they needed food and his mother needed help. Maybe Mrs. Lieberman could help her. He knew that he couldn't take care of his siblings forever.

"Mrs. Huang?"

Mrs. Lieberman's face changed at the sight of his mother. It was frozen in a concerned frown and her tone was stern.

"Mrs. Huang!" she said loudly. Winston's mother jolted awake, gazing up at the woman.

"Mrs. Huang, are you unwell?"

Winston's mother nodded and beckoned for Winston to come to her. He hesitated, and Mrs. Lieberman put her hand on his shoulder. He didn't move.

"I'm Selena Lieberman. I'm here to help you and your children. I will be taking them with me today, and someone will be here shortly to take you to a hospital."

Winston's mother nodded again, and for the first time Winston realized how alone he was. His mother wasn't going to do anything to stop someone from taking them away, and his father was not coming back. Just then his younger sister, Amy, age three, toddled into the living room. Mrs. Lieberman knelt down again to speak to Winston. "How many children live in this house?"

"Four," he replied softly. "It's me, my brother, Josh, my sister Amy, and my baby brother, Jack."

Amy came over and hugged Winston, then looked up at him and said, "Hungry; I am hungry, Winston."

Winston looked down at her. She had no idea they would be leaving soon and that they may not see their parents for a long time.

"Winston, can you wake the other children up? I'm going to make some phone calls so we can help your mother, and then I'll talk to you all together."

Winston nodded solemnly, and then headed to the back of the apartment with Amy trailing behind him. He woke Josh up first, who immediately started toward the kitchen.

"Hold on," Winston said, grabbing the back of his shirt. "Mommy's not feeling well and there's a lady here to help her."

Josh looked up at him, "What lady? Where?"

"She's in the living room. We're going to leave soon. She's going to take us somewhere else."

"I don't want to go!" Josh stomped his feet and started to cry, which woke Jack up in his crib and he started to cry too. Then Amy, not wanting to feel left out, began crying as well.

Winston heard steps down the hall and soon Mrs. Lieberman stood in the doorway.

"Well hello, what's all this crying?" She knelt down again and smiled at Josh and Amy.

"I don't want to go!" Josh repeated.

"I know. I understand, but it's not safe for you to be here anymore. We're going to find you someplace clean where there is plenty of food to eat and an adult to take care of you."

It's strange that sometimes you get so used to a place that you can't see it for what it is. Winston never thought of their home as particularly dirty, but as he looked around the room he shared with his siblings, he started to see the stains on the walls and the mold in the corners. His mother hadn't done laundry in a while so the sheets weren't as white as they used to be. And there were cobwebs in the window frames. Maybe their house was dirty. Was that bad? Is that why they had to leave? Did that make them dirty too?

Mrs. Lieberman helped them pack their things. He heard other voices coming from the living room. "That's just the police officer," Mrs. Lieberman explained. "He's here to help you too." She shut the door to their room so he couldn't hear anything anymore. By the time they were all packed, his mother was gone from her chair in the living room. Winston held Josh and Amy's hands, and Mrs. Lieberman carried Jack as they left their apartment for the last time.

———

The four Huang children were placed in separate foster care homes.

Jack, being a baby, was adopted almost immediately. Josh and Amy were placed together in a home about an hour away from where Winston was placed. Of the three new families, Winston's was the worst. His foster father insisted on strict adherence to his rules, and would enforce those rules with harsh physical punishments. His foster mother worked nights and slept through most of the day. When she was around, she was deferential to her husband and never even attempted to shield the children from his abuse.

By the time he was in high school, Winston had hardened from the eight year old who cared for his siblings and kissed his mother goodnight. He dreamt of the day he would be emancipated from the system. He would serve his mandatory military year and rise up through the ranks. And if he felt like it, he would come back and beat the shit out of his foster father for all he had put him through. Winston would go to sleep dreaming of his future military glory, and of his revenge. By the time he graduated high school, it was 2023. The country was becoming ever more divided on racial and socioeconomic lines, and the sentiment which would spark the 2025 riots was beginning to build.

———

May 10, 2024

"Are you serious, dude?"

Two teenaged boys were standing in an alley outside of a bar. It was two o'clock in the morning. Winston was one, and the other was his friend T.J.

"So what? He's just some fucking faggot."

Winston was holding a pistol, cocked at the ready and aimed at another boy who was lying on the ground in the fetal position, having already been beaten.

"C'mon, dude. He didn't mean anything by it. We only have a week left here and then our mandatory year is over. Let's just go. He won't tell anyone."

Winston knelt down close to the beaten boy's ear, "Will you tell anyone about tonight? You just got too drunk and fell down a few times. You didn't beat me at darts, call me a loser, and then get the shit kicked out of you, right?"

The boy shook his head.

"All right then, we'll let you live."

Winston spat on his face as the boy turned over, trying to get up. T.J. ran down the alley and out on the street. Winston strode slowly behind him, his chest up and his head high. No one would mess with him anymore. Those days were over.

———

After his mandatory year, Winston formally joined the U.S. Army. He was stationed in a newly- built base outside of Detroit. He was still in touch with his siblings, all three of whom were living in suburbs outside of Chicago. Josh was fifteen, Amy was fourteen, and Jack was eleven. He and Amy had stayed the closest. She was always sympathetic to the pain he endured at the hands of his foster father, and she simply missed her big brother.

After spending two months on base, he was sent to do a tour in the former state of Iraq which was going through its own redefining stage. The Iraqi Kurds had finally declared formal independence in 2018, which had lasted for two years before another sectarian civil war had broken out. By 2024, things were finally quieting down as the new states of Kurdistan and South Iraq held their first elections.

The U.S. was sending in a new wave of troops to maintain order during the elections in South Iraq. Kurdistan was unified, but South Iraq was made up of Sunnis and Shiites, as well as numerous other smaller tribal groups, and a fairly large population of Kurds who had chosen to remain there. Winston had very little knowledge of these tribal intricacies, but his experiences there helped define his view of democracy and of war. He was there for nine months, watching the elections and new government unfold.

There was an entire generation of Iraqis who had never known their country without the presence of U.S. troops and ongoing conflict. They were war weary and ready for some sense of stability from the new government. This stability took the form of strict rules and policies. To avoid random acts of violence, a curfew was enacted and a coalition of South Iraqi and U.S. troops were constantly monitoring their assigned neighborhoods.

Winston learned first-hand how to maintain order in a country recovering from civil war; a country made newly independent with their former fellow citizens next door. He also saw those orphaned by war trying to find access to education and jobs in a top down economy that was experimenting with capitalism. He saw himself in the faces of teenage boys who only knew how to survive hand to mouth, and brandish a weapon when threatened. By the time he returned to Detroit, protests had begun. He maintained the stern face of a loyal military man at first but deep down he was on the side of the working man, the proletariat.

———

June 30, 2025

"Winston, I'll need you to bring in the ammunition."

"Yes, sir."

"You can get it from the base without suspicion?"

"Easily, there is so much going in and out of that place no one will be the wiser."

Winston had met the leader of the protesters, Steve Houston, at a bar near the base about a month after he got back from South Iraq. Already, Winston had begun to sympathize with the people in Detroit. He saw in this city the same system which had failed to take care of him as an orphaned eight-year-old boy. The government was taking advantage of poor, disenfranchised people. So when Steve had talked to him about joining a group of anti-government protesters, he agreed.

A couple months later, he had asked Winston about the ammunition. It was long known that the military didn't keep meticulous records when it came to its weapons and ammunition inventories.

Steve was gathering a militia to storm the Capitol Building. They would take it by force, allow civilians to leave, and occupy the building until the government agreed to their terms. He also explained to Winston that he and his team had planted bombs underneath four train stations and they were planning to detonate them one by one if their demands were not met.

"Okay, so you will deliver the first round of ammunition to me on Thursday, and then bring the rest of it to Luke on Monday, the morning of the attack. Those fuckers will lose a whole week and miss several votes on key legislation...especially the census bill."

Winston nodded. "Yes, sir."

"So, do you have any fun weekend plans?"

"Excuse me?"

"For the Fourth of July, Independence Day. Ironic isn't it? They get back from a holiday weekend celebrating independence only to have theirs taken away."

Steve chuckled at his own joke, but Winston said nothing. He liked Steve, and he believed in the movement, but sometimes his blunt nature and propensity for violence reminded him of his foster father.

———

July 7, 2025

The morning of the attack, Winston was not on duty—a lucky coincidence which would work in his favor. If he had requested the day off, or feigned an illness, it could have aroused suspicion. This way, the military would be none the wiser. His instructions were to meet Luke and a dozen or so other recruits in the basement of a house ten blocks from the Capitol Building at dawn.

That morning he left while it was still dark. He cut through neighborhood yards to save time. The morning air was cold, and dew resting on the blades of grass fell on his shoes as he walked. He was lost in his thoughts and arrived at the house quicker than he expected. What was even more unexpected was who he saw when he got there.

He didn't believe it was her at first. Her black bobbed hair and small frame stood out among the large men in the basement. She turned when he entered, and though he was shocked to see her in this setting, she seemed to be expecting him.

"Amy? What are you doing here?"

Amy smiled mischievously. "I'm here for the revolution."

He motioned for her to come closer so they could speak in semi-privacy. "How did you get here from Chicago? Do your foster parents know about this?"

"First of all, I took the train. I'm not a child anymore, I can buy a ticket. And secondly, of course Hank and Anne don't know. Are you kidding? They think I'm sleeping over at Sharon's house."

"This isn't safe, Amy. These people have real weapons. You shouldn't be here."

Amy looked up at him defiantly. "You're here."

"Yes, and I'm in the Army. I've been trained."

"Yeah, in the Army but helping these people."

"One has nothing to do with the other. We're protesting the state government at the Capitol Building. I work for the federal government."

"Oh really? I don't think your commanding officers would see it that way."

She was right but Winston would never admit that. He narrowed his gaze. "We are not having this conversation any more. Go home, Amy. It's not safe here. How did you even hear about this?"

Amy smiled as she looked over at a young man with shaggy blonde hair. "Luke told me about it. We were both at the library during study hall and we started talking."

"Study hall? He's in high school?" Winston glanced over at Luke. His hair hung almost to his shoulders. He wore jeans, a grey hooded sweatshirt, and black combat boots. He was taller and broader than Winston and by the way Steve had talked about him, he had assumed Luke was older, in his mid-twenties.

"He's only two years younger than you, calm down. And he just graduated. He moved here to stay with his cousin, Steve, over the summer before his mandatory year starts."

Winston inhaled sharply. "Amy, I'm not asking you. I'm telling you. Go back to the station and get on the first train back to Chicago."

Luke had moved closer to them by this point. "Everything all right over here? You okay, Amy?"

Winston wanted to strangle this little miscreant but he kept his cool. "We're fine. Actually, she's my sister. We haven't seen each other in a while so we were just catching up."

"No shit, seriously? That's crazy. Well I'm glad we're all here together then."

Amy smiled and moved closer to Luke, who put his arm around her shoulders, and she smiled at Winston while replying, "Yes, I'm fine. Thanks, babe."

Luke addressed Winston, "So you must be Winston Huang, the guy with the ammunition, right?"

Winston nodded.

"Steve showed me your picture so I'd know. Okay, cool. The weapons we're using are all on those tables in the corner. Steve said to organize the correct ammunition with the weapons. Do you want some help with that or you just want to unload the stuff?"

"I'll do it," Winston said abruptly. When he got to the tables, he shook his head and started unloading ammunition from a bag he had secured around his waist. He had also hidden some in the inside pockets of his jacket. Having Amy here was a complication he did not expect. He sighed. Just as he was finishing up, the door opened again and it was Steve.

"So, are we all set in here?" His tone was serious, but he looked almost jovial. Winston knew that feeling; when all your plans are set for an ambush there is a sense of excitement, and also some relief. The planning is over; now the fun can begin.

Steve and Winston loaded the weapons together, passing them around to the group of over thirty militia members gathered in the basement. They were one of five groups, according to Steve, and they had contacts inside the Capitol Building. Only men who had completed their mandatory year and women who had served were armed. That was Steve's rule, but somehow he had waved it when it came to Luke.

"I trained him myself, this summer," Steve commented as he passed Luke a hunting rifle with an impressive scope.

As they started to leave the basement, Winston moved closer to Amy. "Stay next to me, please. I know what I'm doing. I can protect you if this gets out of hand." Amy opened her mouth to speak but closed it and nodded in agreement when she saw the stern look on Winston's face.

They headed out toward the Capitol Building. Winston would be one of the look outs, stationed a couple blocks away. The other groups, around one hundred fifty people in all, would take the Capitol Building, easily overpowering the handful of guards on duty. The protests that had been going on for the past month had been nonviolent. This militia would catch the government off guard, or so they thought.

As they got closer to the building something felt off to Winston. They were in sight of it and no one was there. It was nearly 8:00 am; government workers should be arriving by now.

Steve held his hand up to stop the group, and then turned to Winston. "Okay, you stay here."

"It's too quiet, Steve. It's almost like they're expecting us."

Steve shook his head and put his hand on Winston's shoulder. "Don't worry. I've been in these situations before. I would know if there was a problem."

Steve turned back around and motioned for the rest of the militia to follow him. They marched proudly toward the Capitol Building. The four other groups appeared from other streets near the building and joined up with them. They were at least a hundred strong. Steve was at the front and Luke was slightly behind him, to his left. Amy stayed back with Winston, crouched down low next to him. Winston's pulse quickened. He could feel his heart pounding in his chest. As the group approached the building, armed men poured out of the main entrance encircling the perimeter.

"What's happening? Who are those people?" Amy whispered.

"We need to go back. They've been outed. Someone knew they were coming. This could get out of hand. You have to get out of here."

"No. I won't leave without Luke, what if he…"

Just then Luke emerged from the militia group, pulled his rifle up to his shoulder and fired directly at the entrance. Two men dropped to the ground, either hit by the bullet and shrapnel, or dodging it. Another man stepped forward, raised his military grade rifle and shot Luke in the shoulder, and before Winston could stop her Amy ran out yelling, "Luke, no!"

She made it within a block of the building when the same man who had shot Luke fired again, this time hitting Amy in the forehead. Her body dropped to the ground instantly. She was dead.

The world swirled around Winston. His vision became blurry; he felt nauseous. He started to stumble forward toward Amy's body. Everyone was firing their weapons now. He smelled smoke in the air. It was a full out battle. With the sound of gunfire, his military training kicked in and he began to focus. He got to where Amy had fallen but saw that someone was carrying her body away. He tried to scream but no one could hear him over the gunfire. Then he looked up and saw the gunman who had shot her. He was moving carefully down the stairs of the Capitol, firing into the militia. He was tall, barrel chested and well-groomed. His dark brown hair and neatly-trimmed beard framed his face. Winston started to charge toward him when someone grabbed his shirt and yanked him backwards. It was Steve.

"Get out of here; go take care of your sister. I'll deal with George Adams."

"Who is George Adams?" Winston asked, breathlessly.

"The shooter."

———

There were dozens of casualties of the attempted storming of the Capitol Building. Luke survived, but Amy was accompanied in death by many others on both sides. Steve was captured and interrogated. He disclosed the location of the train station bombs and they were dismantled. Months of rioting followed, and eventually some concessions were made to the protesters and the city moved on. The 2025 riots had made their mark, but no great revolution had happened.

George Adams would have no memory of Winston's face. To him, he was only another terrorist attempting to take the Capitol. Winston, however, remembered George quite clearly. He watched him become Attorney General and then Governor of Michigan. He kept a close eye on George Adams right up until he murdered him in 2056, shooting him in the chest, next to Ambassador Bridge, in the first months of the revolution.

March 12, 2056

"General Huang, sir. We're ready when you are."

Winston strode over to the door. He had done everything he had promised himself he would do, justice was in sight, and he was about to formally announce that he was the leader of the revolution.

He had learned to control his anger while in uniform. He would have never made it to where he was now if he hadn't. The military had a very low tolerance for public displays of violence within its ranks, especially at home. He had seen the images from Abu Ghraib prison at the turn of the century; prisoners on leashes, and American guards with sick, sadistic looks on their faces. The entire military establishment had done an about face after that. They wanted to be seen as protectors, not torturers and goons.

Winston had gone along with all that in theory, but he was known as a harsh interrogator when someone resisted the traditional techniques. He was never suspected of participating in the 2025 riots. That part of his past, along with other transgressions, was never discovered. He always had the fire for social justice and revolution inside him though and by 2056 he was finally in a position to do something about it.

He had organized a coup d'état. It had not been difficult. The government was so corrupt that the civilian population was already on the verge of revolt. Who could blame them? The economic inequalities were staggering, and they were herded like cattle after being priced out of their homes. He knew those areas of Detroit personally, but it was happening all over the country, especially in his hometown of Chicago. Yes, it was time for real change and Winston Huang would be the man to lead it, just as he had always dreamed.

He was festooned in all his military regalia. His jacket had been tailored to fit like a glove. This was Winston at his finest, the best version of himself. He nodded to the guard and motioned for him to open the door. "I'm ready," he said. "Let's begin."

Emily's Resolution

Emily could hear her heartbeat in her ears, pounding methodically with every step she took. She was gripping her mother's hand, pulling her forward with every bound. They were running, breathless, through the streets of Detroit, following John Caring. Ambulance sirens wailed, drowning out the sound of his voice. He was motioning to turn left at the next street. They were heading west. Did he have a plan? He must have some plan as to where they would go, but what would they do when they got there? They had fled the courthouse so quickly she hadn't thought through the next steps. All of a sudden it became clear; they were going to their old house.

"Dad!"

John Caring stopped and looked back at Emily.

"We can't go to the house. Someone else lives there now."

He looked at her as if he hadn't quite understood what she said and then chuckled, "We're not going in the house, don't worry. We're going someplace much safer."

They had all stopped now.

"John, what if they've moved it? Or what if the code has changed?"

Emily and Wallace looked at each other, confused.

Wallace spoke first, "What are you talking about, Mom? What code? The code to the garage?"

"No, dear, not the garage," Catherine replied, then turned to John. "If Huang is looking for you, he would go to the house first, don't you think?"

"What the hell are you talking about?" Emily demanded.

"There's a bunker underneath the shed behind the house. We had it installed when they first started working on the Ultimate Ending Project. If it fell into the wrong hands, we would be safe, at least for a month or so until the supplies ran out."

Emily's gaze narrowed. "Who else knows about it? Does Rosenthal know?"

"Yes, but only your mother and I know the code. That way, if something happened to me, she could get you kids in there safely."

Catherine looked away. She had told Rosenthal the code soon after they had installed the bunker, when they were having their affair before the war. If something happened to John, she wanted Rosenthal to be safe, with her. She thought she could trust him.

"It's our best bet, and there is communication equipment down there too. We can try to get through to someone in Northwest America or even President Warren. My intel on the project is invaluable."

They all nodded and continued on toward to the house. After almost an hour of walking, they arrived. The house was boarded up; the windows shuttered.

"I thought you said someone was living here?"

"That's what I was told. Ben said he looked it up and a family was registered here."

Catherine looked warily up at the house, "John, I'm not sure about this..."

"Let's just go around the back and see."

They all followed him to the back of the house. The shed was gone. It was just a grassy lawn.

"There's another entrance through the basement."

"John, what if someone is already down there?"

"Who would be down there? You didn't tell anyone the code, and neither did I. Did you?"

Catherine shook her head. She couldn't be certain that Rosenthal was in there. There was so much chaos after the explosion in the courtroom that she hadn't seen where he had gone. He might be dead. They followed John to the back entrance of the house and down the stairs to the basement. It was unfinished, empty, and dark. As they stepped on the cement floors their footsteps echoed.

John went to the back wall and placed his hand in the center. It lit up in a pale green and then a small opening appeared to the left of his hand. There was a numbered key pad. He typed in five numbers and stepped back. The wall slid open along the right side and a door appeared behind it. He walked up and opened the door.

Emily was right behind him. As she entered the bunker, her eyes widened and she gasped. There, seated in the bunker, were Rosenthal and Ben. The color drained from John Caring's face. He turned back and looked at Catherine who stood stone faced behind Emily, and then he sighed heavily, as if the truth he had always suspected about his wife was now attempting to crush him. Then he looked back at Rosenthal. His eyes lit up and his voice was filled with rancor. "What the hell are you doing here?"

Rosenthal stood up. "Now John, be careful. We're armed."

"You're armed. Why? Who else knows the code?"

"No one that I'm aware of, but we can't take any chances. We can all stay here safely, if you agree to remain calm."

"You're telling me what to do in my own house? I built this bunker for my family, for our safety, not yours. I don't know how you got in here, though I can guess, but after you left me in prison for years, and then even when you ousted Huang and took control, you put me on trial. On trial, Isaac! You know damn well what went on before the revolution. We weren't just colleagues, we were friends!"

Rosenthal nodded. "Yes, I understand that, but there are bigger issues now. Please, come inside and let's figure out how to move forward. We can discuss the past later."

John looked back at his family, motioned them forward, and once everyone was inside he closed the door to the bunker and the wall slid shut behind it.

"Okay, I'm going to do the talking now. We need to make contact with the United North, and Northwest America. Huang may have contacted them about the bombs, but they don't know we're down here, safe, and that I have information about the Ultimate Ending Project."

Rosenthal cleared his throat. "Well actually, John, Ben already called his father who spoke with President Warren. His father is Isaiah Hughes, the United North's Ambassador to Lebanon. They're aware that we're down here. And as for the project, I've been collecting an archive of information about it and we were just preparing a briefing sheet for the President. You're welcome to help us, if you'd like."

John Caring was fuming, breathing heavily. "So it looks like you have it covered then. You have the connections, you know about the project, and you've been screwing my wife!"

Catherine gasped, "John, please. It wasn't like that."

Wallace and Emily moved back, behind Catherine, and Ben focused on the typing he was doing on Rosenthal's device.

"Stay out of this, Catherine, you've gone through enough. I don't blame you." Then John turned to Rosenthal. "But you! How could do this to me?"

"John, I don't think you want to talk about this in front of your children."

"Well I don't have any choice, do I? I was in prison, then I was on trial, and now I'm down here, in this bunker, with you."

Rosenthal didn't respond immediately, leaving a thick, tense silence in the air. Then the bunker's phone rang. Ben looked at it. "It's my father."

Rosenthal nodded at him, and Ben answered the phone.

"Hello? Yes. No, John Caring and his family are here now too. Yes, we're preparing it right now and we're going to send it to you and President Warren. Okay, thank you, Dad."

Ben nodded as he was typing, adding the occasional, "Yes, I got it." After several minutes of this, he put the device down. "Thank you so much. I will. Good bye."

Ben hung up the phone and looked up, making eye contact first with Emily. She looked away, and then he looked to Rosenthal and John Caring. "Okay so my Dad confirmed that Michael and Isabelle Stevenson broke into the prison and freed Huang and Mocerino. The United North was able to hack into the surveillance system. The Stevensons used chemical weapons and killed several guards. It was ugly. They don't know where they are, but they're using all the satellites and drones that were available to the United States before the war. They've contacted interim President Harper and she's safe. They've also been in touch with President Joyce of Northwest America, and President Remning of the Confederacy; Texas wants nothing to do with this, but they send their best."

"So is anyone mobilizing ground troops?" Wallace asked.

"Yes, Northwest America is sending in troops to help in the search. They couldn't have gotten very far in a few hours, even if they have access to a car. All air traffic has been halted."

"So where do you think they are?"

Ben shook his head. "I don't know." He looked at Rosenthal, John Caring, and then Wallace and Emily. No one spoke for a moment. Each of them was assessing the situation and searching for its meaning for them individually and collectively.

Emily gazed straight ahead, her eyes unfocused, her thoughts had been swirling within her and now she was organizing them. She had been looking at everyone in the bunker while Ben was on the phone with his father and they all seemed foreign to her. She didn't truly know any of them, even her own parents. Wallace was the same but at the same time he was different too. He had grown up apart from her. During her time in the refugee camp, she had thought a lot about her family and friends. After the war, would they be different? Would she be different? She had a nagging feeling the whole time that there had been more going on before the war than she had understood.

Over the last few months, things had become clearer to her, especially when she was in prison. And now, after everything was revealed in the trial and in the bunker, a stark reality hit her. She could not trust her parents or any of the people she had looked up to in their generation, those she had grown up idolizing, to do the right the thing. Her father was corrupt, her mother was a liar, Rosenthal was a power-hungry egomaniac, and the Stevensons were terrorists. She had listened to them and taken their advice, and the whole time they were only thinking about themselves.

Now, to save her country, she had to take charge. "I think I know where the Stevensons went with Huang."

Rosenthal hurried to her side. "You do? Where?"

Emily eyed him warily. "I don't want you to be involved."

"Now you listen here, I'm the Attorney General. I have a direct line to President Warren. I'm in charge here."

"No, Ben has a direct line to President Warren. You're just some government leech who slept with my mother and persecuted my father. I'll decide who I'm working with, not you."

"Why you little bitch!"

Wallace moved closer to Emily, but she didn't glance back at him. Her eyes narrowed as she looked at Rosenthal with contempt. "You can call me names and yell at me all you want. I don't want you to be a part of this."

Rosenthal took a step back, trying to regain his composure. "All right, I can see you're serious. I'm sorry. I just want us all to be clear on what information you have so we can assess the situation accurately. We can work on this together, as a team."

Emily shook her head. "No, the only team I'm on is with my family, and Ben; no one else."

Ben looked shocked, he thought for sure she wouldn't want him involved. Then again, he did have the direct line to President Warren through his father. That was probably why she wanted him.

John, Catherine, and Wallace crowded around Emily, who whispered in Catherine's ear.

"Remember the Stevensons' vacation house on Mackinac Island? That's where I think they are."

Catherine nodded.

"What is this? You're actually whispering the information now?" Rosenthal said, then he looked to Catherine with pleading eyes. "Catherine, be reasonable. You know the information I have is *invaluable* to stopping the project from going any further."

John started to speak, but Emily interrupted him. "No, don't talk to her like that. I'm leading this team."

Everyone turned to look at her, but Ben spoke first, "Emily, I understand why you don't want Rosenthal involved. I understand why you don't trust him, and I know you only want me for my connections, but Rosenthal does know more about the project than anyone here. His information is valuable. I have some familiarity with it, but he's been studying it for years. You can leave him here if you want to, but if we find them, you may wish you had him with us."

Emily considered this, and then said, "Okay, but I want him searched first. He can't have any weapons. Wallace, can you search him?"

Wallace brushed past her and began frisking Rosenthal. He found two knives and a gun. All standard military issue from his mandatory year. He handed them to Emily, who put one knife in her boot, handed one knife to her mother, and then gave the gun back to Wallace. "You know how to use this better than I do, you take it," and then she glanced at Rosenthal, "Use it on him if you have to."

"So where are we going?" asked Rosenthal.

"Mackinac Island, the Stevensons have a vacation home there. I think that's where they went."

"We have to alert the President."

"No. What don't you get about this? You're not in charge any more. If they see a bunch of helicopters and troops, they could get spooked and Huang could set off another bomb, and if they go in there with a drone strike, they could end up blowing up the entire New Republic. Who knows what chemicals they have in there? They

226

won't be expecting us. I know that neighborhood very well. I used to go there on vacation with the Stevensons when I was a kid. Once we arrive, and confirm that they are there, then we can contact the President for back up."

Then she addressed Ben, "Are you almost done with the briefing of the project?"

Ben sat down and started typing, "Almost, just a couple more minutes."

"Okay when you're done send it to your father. I don't want them suspecting that you're up to anything. I assume you drove here since you both got here first?"

Ben nodded.

"Give me the keys."

Ben tossed her the car keys that were sitting on the desk in front of him.

"All right, everyone clear on the plan?"

They all nodded.

Ben tapped quickly on his device and then stood up when the briefing had been sent, "All done."

"Okay, let's go."

John ran up to the keypad and typed in the code. The door opened, and they all followed Emily out of the bunker. Wallace took up the rear, his gun raised to Rosenthal's back. When they got to the car, Emily opened the doors with Rosenthal's keys.

"There isn't room for everyone in here," she said, then motioned to Wallace. "Put him in the trunk."

Rosenthal grimaced, but with Wallace's gun raised he obeyed silently, climbing into the trunk. Wallace closed the trunk and put the gun in his waistband.

"Mom, I think you should ride up front with me. You've been up to Mackinac Island several times, do you remember the terrain?"

Catherine nodded. "Yes, very well."

"Okay, good."

They all got in the car. Emily in the driver's seat, Catherine in the passenger's seat, and John, Wallace, and Ben in the back. They took several side streets until they got onto the highway. It would take nearly six hours to drive there and they couldn't waste any time. If Huang held true to his threat, he would detonate another bomb somewhere in the world in fifteen hours.

They had been driving for just over an hour when John leaned forward, "What if they closed the bridge?"

Emily nodded, considering this. "Then we'll just have to re-open it. Ben, do you think you could handle that? You are an engineer."

"I guess I'll have to."

Wallace shook his head, "I don't think they'd close the bridge. That would be too obvious. Someone would notice that there were people on the island who shouldn't be there. If anything, I bet they rigged it with C4."

"You're probably right son, good thinking," John replied.

For many years the only way to get to Mackinac Island was to take a ferry from Mackinaw City. Then, during the post-2025 rebuilding and subsequent tourism boom, a bridge had been built to Mackinac Island. There was also a ten-minute private airplane ride available by reservation. During the war, Mackinac Island had been evacuated and no one had been relocated there. It was a ghost town, more or less.

They drove on, pulling over once to get some food from a gas station and to check on Rosenthal in the trunk. He was fine—nauseous and slightly disoriented, but uninjured. Once they were within an hour from Mackinaw City, Emily began to get nervous. Everything had seemed so clear to her down in the bunker. This was what she had to do, take charge. These people had to be stopped.

Now that they were closer, she started thinking about Annabelle and Christopher. Michael and Isabelle were their parents and now they were criminals. What if they had to injure them or worse? She had spent plenty of time in prison thinking about all of these people, the ones in the car with her now, the Stevensons, and the children in her class. What world would they grow up in? This was the right thing to do, but did she have what it would take to see it through?

Finally, they pulled into Mackinaw City, about a mile from the bridge, just as the sun was setting. Emily parked in the parking lot of an abandoned building at the edge of the city. She saw buildings in the distance, punctuating a clear skyline.

"I think we should walk from here. They could be monitoring the bridge."

John nodded, and Wallace went to the trunk to get Rosenthal. He tumbled out of the back and was unsteady on his feet at first, but eventually he began to walk normally.

They walked together silently, all following Emily through the woods until they got close enough to the bridge that they could see the shoreline. Wallace moved over to Emily's far left so he could get a better view of the underside of the bridge.

"Yep," he nodded, whispering to Emily, "I can see the C4 under the bridge. There's a ton of it."

There were a couple old power boats on the shoreline. Emily turned to Wallace. "We will wait for a couple hours, well past nightfall, and then take one of the boats across."

"Will that give us enough time?"

"It will have to; it's the only way for us to get across undetected."

A few hours later, Emily led them down to the shore and they all climbed into the power boat furthest from the bridge. She rummaged through different compartments near the steering wheel until she found the key. "Who knows how to drive a power boat?"

John stepped up. "I do, give me the key."

He revved up the engine, turned the boat around, and drove them across until they reached the island. No one spoke. In fact, no one had really spoken except Wallace and Emily since they had gotten to Mackinaw City. The dynamics had shifted amongst them so dramatically that they were the only two who felt it was safe to speak.

After they disembarked, Emily needed to get her bearings. She asked Catherine for guidance and soon they were only two blocks from the Stevensons' vacation home. Sure enough, there was a car parked out front. Emily's heart began to beat rapidly as the adrenaline pumped through her veins. Then she felt someone close to her and she tensed up. It was Ben.

"It looks like they're here. Should I tell my father?"

Emily nodded, "Yes, tell him we're in position but not to send in anyone yet. We need to secure them, not spook them."

Ben pulled out his device and tapped rapidly, sending the quick and urgent message.

Emily motioned for them to gather around her. "Okay, we need to go around back and figure out where they are in the house...then I will go in alone and assess the situation. Then I'll signal for you to come join me. Got it?"

Just then Ben's device lit up. It was a message from his father. A bomb had gone off in Tokyo. They couldn't be sure it was Huang but that was their suspicion.

Ben had read the message aloud, and after he was done Emily motioned for him to pass her his device. She looked down at the screen, reading each word cautiously as if any sudden movement could set off another bomb. If the Tokyo bomb was the work of Huang, then he most likely had panicked and set off the bomb earlier than his announced timeline to keep anyone from trying to catch him and to hurry the government's submission to his demands.

Emily sighed, handing the device to Wallace who passed it back to

Ben.

"We will proceed as planned. They have to be stopped."

Everyone nodded.

They moved closer to the Stevensons' house and then they crouched down low behind the bushes that were in front of the house next door. Emily crept up along the side of the house until she reached the back window, which looked into the kitchen. She rose slowly until she could see through the window. She steadied her breathing as she took in the scene. Michael and Isabelle Stevenson, and Huang were all seated at the kitchen table. They were gathered around Huang's device, all concentrating intently on what was on the screen. Their backs were to her, so Emily couldn't see everything on the screen, but it looked like a map. There was a back door that led to the kitchen. That would be how they would enter to confront them. Emily crept back around and motioned for Wallace, Ben, Rosenthal, and her parents to come join her.

Wallace was the only one who was armed, so he came up closest to her with his gun at the ready.

"I'll go in first and you follow behind me," he whispered to Emily.

Once they were next to the back door, Emily nodded to Wallace and he leapt up and opened the door with his gun raised. Emily followed behind him, with Ben behind her. John, Catherine, and Rosenthal stood just outside the doorway.

Huang dropped his device on the table, and he and the Stevensons froze.

"We are here to detain you until the authorities arrive. President

Warren and President Joyce have sent ground troops to surround the house, and helicopters will be here any minute to take you in. If you try to run, the snipers will shoot you. It's as simple as that."

Huang sneered at Emily, "Silly girl. Do you think I was not prepared for this? The bombs will go off as planned unless I, personally, shut them down. Without me to stop them, these bombs will destroy entire countries. You need to take me alive and uninjured, and I need to agree to cooperate with you."

"What about them? The Stevensons will be killed if you don't co-operate."

Huang chuckled, "I only needed them to free me and connect me with the Ultimate Ending Project. They're disposable, just like any of the other scientists I've worked with."

Neither of the Stevensons looked at Huang after he said this, they were both frozen.

"Where is the project?"

Huang was silent. Emily looked at Michael and Isabelle, "Where is it?"

They didn't answer her.

"Tell me where it is!"

Suddenly her father was at her side. "That's enough of this. Let's take them into custody, and then President Warren can sort them out. There are interrogation specialists for this."

Emily nodded and then turned to Ben. "Can you find something to tie them up with?"

Ben hurried to the kitchen cabinets and started opening them, eventually finding some kitchen twine and a pair of scissors.

Wallace kept his gun raised as Emily instructed each of their prisoners to stand, and then Ben tied their hands behind their backs. They all filed out of the house and into the back yard, and Ben picked up Huang's device from the table.

"Now we wait," Emily said under her breath.

They were standing in the back yard. Wallace kept his gun raised at the prisoners. No one spoke. The silence was deafening, and the air was tense.

Then John said, "Isaac, tell everyone here the truth. Tell them what you really knew before the war; tell them what we were planning. Tell them the truth."

Rosenthal shook his head. "It's over John. Just let it go."

"No, it's not over. My trial was interrupted, I wasn't acquitted."

"I'll drop the charges, just let it go now."

John gasped, "You'll drop the charges will you? Well isn't that nice of you. What about my reputation? What job will I get when this is all over? What about my relationship with my wife? I can't rejoin my family, not in the same way." Then John pulled out a gun he had concealed in his jacket and pointed it at Rosenthal.

"Dad, what are you doing?" Emily screamed.

John acted like he didn't hear her, "You thought I wasn't armed, that

I was helpless. Well I took this from the bailiff after he was knocked down from the explosion at the courthouse. Now, tell them."

Rosenthal's eyes were wide. "Why? What good would it do? The project will be over soon. Hell, the New Republic may be over soon."

John moved closer now so his gun was almost touching Rosenthal's forehead. "I'll decide what good it would do, tell them."

"John, please..."

"Tell them or I'll shoot you in the head!" John was shaking with rage.

Rosenthal lunged at him, knocking him to the ground. The gun flew through the air and landed a few feet from them. Rosenthal went to grab it and John grabbed his ankle, pulling him to the ground. Rosenthal inched himself forward on his stomach until he had hold of the gun, then turned and shot at John, barely missing him.

Wallace began to panic, pointing his gun at Rosenthal, and then Huang and the Stevensons, and then back at Rosenthal.

Emily moved behind their scuffle with her knife raised, trying to find a moment to stab Rosenthal so she could get the gun.

Everything was happening so fast. Catherine was screaming. Ben was moving toward the scuffle. Then the gun went off again and John Caring lay crumpled on the ground, blood oozing from his temple. Emily lunged forward and stabbed Rosenthal in the back. He screamed out in pain and dropped the gun. She ran forward, grabbed the gun and held it up to Rosenthal's head.

Tears were welling up in her eyes, but she held her focus. She stood up slowly, keeping the gun aimed at Rosenthal. Her gaze narrowed as she circled him until their eyes locked.

She spat out her words like venom, "What were your plans for the project?"

His face was streaked with sweat and dirt, and he was breathing heavily. His hand was pressed against his stab wound. He gave out a labored moan.

Emily kept the gun raised and said very quietly, "Tell me what you were planning."

"We were… I was planning on selling parts of the project to a terrorist organization in Prague called Svoboda."

Emily's eyes widened. "Why? What would you gain?"

"They're a progressive organization. They were going to help me take over. Detroit was going to hell in a handbasket before the war, and so was the rest of the country. We had to do something. These people are visionaries. Your father knew about my plan, but he didn't like the Svoboda, so he found a different, less militant organization in Paris. We were partners. We worked on everything together. Then the war broke out and everything was too unstable for any sale to go through. I was waiting for things to settle down, and then I was going to go through with it on my own, my deal with Svoboda. That's why I put John on trial, to get him out of the way. He always thought he knew what was best. If my plan had worked, I could have secured the New Republic, gotten the rest of The Five to submit to my terms, and I would have become the new leader of the free world."

Rosenthal was gasping for breath now. The color was draining from his face. He was bleeding out. Emily didn't know how much longer he would live.

"So my father tried to stop the deal with Svoboda?"

Rosenthal nodded, and then his eyes rolled back in his head and his body slumped over, lifeless.

Then they heard helicopters overhead.

Everything after that felt like some strange dream. When Emily remembered that day, everything was hazy and she felt like she was watching it from above. Soldiers dropped from three helicopters. They immediately went to Ben who began explaining and motioning toward Huang and the Stevensons, and Rosenthal's body. Catherine lay over John's body and the soldiers had to pry her off of him, her arms flailing and her grieving wails drowned out by the sounds of helicopter propellers. Two soldiers took Huang and the Stevensons into custody, and they flew off in one helicopter. John Caring and Isaac Rosenthal's bodies were wrapped in blankets and loaded onto another helicopter, and the third took Ben, Wallace, Catherine, and Emily to Washington D.C.

———

July 28, 2061

"Ms. Caring, please tell us, to the best of your recollection, what exactly Isaac Rosenthal said."

Emily was going through her debriefing with President Warren and his head of security. Ben, Wallace, and Catherine were doing the same simultaneously with other members of his security team. She recalled everything she knew about her father's role in the Ultimate Ending Project, from her first meeting with him while he was in prison, up until Rosenthal's dying confession.

Then they asked her various questions about her childhood and she told them what she could remember—her observations, and every conversation with her father. By the end of the day she was exhausted. She was in mourning for her father, but also felt a sense of relief. It was over. She could finally, truly, go home.

Ben handed over Huang's device and the government cryptologists cracked Huang's codes and stopped the upcoming bombs. Huang and the Stevensons were flown to The Hague where they would be tried for their crimes by the International Criminal Court.

―――――

Over the next few weeks, the New Republic quickly crumbled and was absorbed into the United North. Northwest America maintained good terms with the United North, and Texas and the Confederacy were civil. The former United Sates of America became The Four, as it is today.

Epilogue

June 2, 2085

Emily Caring Hughes sat up in bed, watching the minutes tick by, waiting until it was time to get up and start her day. It was her fiftieth birthday. Since it was Saturday, her children, Ely and Daniel, would be sleeping in, or so she thought. Ely was home from college for the summer, and Daniel was heading off to camp in a few weeks. They were both about the same ages Emily and her younger brother Daniel had been when the war had broken out. If her brother was alive, he would be forty-six now. It was strange to think that it was almost thirty years since that day when she had escaped from Aunt Caroline's house into the woods.

The journey from that moment to now had been long and difficult. After the New Republic fell and was absorbed into the United North, she had gone to law school at her father's alma mater, New York University. Ben had joined President Warren's staff in the new capital, New York City. Then they had adopted Ely and Daniel. After spending time away from her family and teaching refugee children in the camp, she knew she wanted to adopt and Ben had agreed. And thus they had created their family. They had stayed in New York until five years ago when Emily had been asked to be a judge at the International Criminal Court. It was a great opportunity and they had agreed it was the right time, so they had moved their family to Geneva. The court itself had moved there after The Four was created. Switzerland continued to be a symbol of peace and stability, and after all the upheaval it had been decided by the powers that be that the court was best stationed there.

They kept their townhouse in New York, and went back as often as they could. That was where she was now, in the same bed where she had read her children bedtime stories, in the same house where she had brought them home. They would be spending the summer there while the court was in recess.

In her role, she oversaw the trials of the greatest war criminals in the world. They had committed crimes against humanity, and for that they must be punished. Emily was stern but fair, and always managed to see the truth through the fog.

There was a knock on her door.

"Mom, are you up? We have a surprise for you." Daniel's voice drifted in, muffled by the door.

"Yes, dear, I'm up."

He opened the door and smiled at her. "Come downstairs, we have a surprise for you."

Emily climbed out of bed, stepped into her slippers, put a robe over her pajamas, and followed him downstairs. He brought her to the dining room, where there was a huge bouquet of white roses in the middle of the table, and streamers and balloons hanging above it. Ben and Ely were standing next to the table.

"Happy Birthday, Mom."

"Happy Birthday, Emily."

Emily smiled. Ely stepped back and pointed to a large framed photo next to the flowers. The frame was beautiful, ornate, silver, and Emily recognized the photo immediately. She rushed over and picked it up. Her eyes widened. She couldn't believe what she saw.

She looked to Ben first. "How did you get this?"

Daniel answered instead, "I found it! They have these archives now of photos that were lost during the war. I guess this was taken in the old Detroit Capitol Building, when Grandpa was the Attorney General."

Tears welled up in Emily's eyes as she looked down at the photo of her family at a Christmas party in 2043. She was eight years old, Daniel was four years old, and Wallace was just a baby. Her mother's hand was on her shoulder and her father was holding Wallace. Then she looked up at her current family, taking in their warm, loving faces, and she whispered, "Thank you."

Photo credit: Scott Cullen

Elizabeth Austin studied international relations in the United States, Scotland, and France. She has traveled to faraway places, and lived to write the tale. She currently resides in Los Angeles.

CPSIA information can be obtained
at www.ICGtesting.com
Printed in the USA
FSOW02n0727040517
33873FS